MAYBE LOVE MAYBE NOT

UDAI YADLA

Contents

Blessed with Love

"Did you hear this, Akash? The neighbour boy, Siddu, committed suicide."

I stared at Payal, my beautiful wife, in horror.

"You heard it right. He wrote a suicide note, saying he is committing suicide because he hated his life and has nothing to live for."

"He never once thought about his poor parents who witnessed his body in two parts on the railway track. What a stupid he is, isn't he?"

I was lost in thoughts. My mind drifted five years back in time.

❧

The rails clamoured under the heavy wheels of the metal giants. The railway's speakers did not spare a moment of silence with incessant announcements. The noisy vendors added to the cacophony of the railway station. I was sitting on a lonely bench, my soulless eyes staring at the busy rails. Even the high decibel noise couldn't disturb my train of thoughts. As I stared at the bustling bevy of trains, I wondered which one would take me to my destination. The cold December breeze made me feel a little chill despite my heavily clad body. As I scanned along the platform towards the far end where the trains leave the platform onto the secluded tracks, I saw an old man shivering in the cold. He folded his legs towards his chest as he sat, wrapping his arms around his legs. I walked to the old man with pitiful eyes. I stared at him for a moment and without a thought, removed my jacket and wrapped it around the old man. The grateful look in the old man's eyes made me somewhat uneasy. I extracted my wallet, peeled out the currency notes, and gave them to the old man, then immediately rushed to my seat without looking back. I resumed my previous posture and continued my observation. As I was lost again in my thoughts, I felt my privacy was intruded.

"May I sit here?" There was a beautiful girl with a sparkling smile asking my permission to sit beside me. She had a fair, flawless face with an innocent smile. Her puppy eyes blinked as a strand of her hair fell in front of her eyes. She walked her petite body a couple of steps towards me with elegance. I was in two minds. My mind warned me not to entertain her, but my heart made me nod my head in an instant. A beautiful woman is such a powerful influence; I couldn't deny. The bustling crowd turned mute for an instant. She sat beside me and shuffled on the seat uneasily. She took a little longer to get settled.

"Maybe she is hesitant. Maybe she wanted something. I don't care." I thought.

She looked around as if searching for something. Occasionally, she stole glances at me. I didn't pay attention.

"Can I borrow your phone for a second?" she asked hesitantly.

I was confused.

"I missed my phone somewhere. I just wanted to try calling it."

I gave the phone to her without looking at her. She immediately called her number. The sound of the phone ringing came from her handbag. She gently knocked herself on her forehead.

"I'm such an absent-minded person," she said and stood up to leave, handing over my phone.

Without even thanking me, she hastily left the spot.

The last few minutes were so bizarre. I recollected what had happened. The lady, so gently, asked for permission to sit beside me. She quickly made an impression. Then she acted crazy and asked for my phone. Then again, she left without even thanking.

"Girls! They make an impression quick; Leave you quicker than that."

"But they leave scars so deep that it stays far longer."

My mind drifted back to my bitter memory.

❧

Life was a beautiful dream.

I waited for her at the KFC restaurant, guessing what could transpire for the day. By the way, I was not holding any good news. I was fired from my job. Of course, I had been irresponsible. I skipped my office to be able to take my girlfriend out for movies and shopping. She was the most important thing in my life. I paid so much attention to her that I had scarce bit of my mind on my job. I recalled the day before when I first missed a rendezvous. I was surrounded by the bosses in a closed conference chamber, meekly defending a volley of questions.

"This is the worst screw-up the company had ever known." my boss shouted, sipping his coffee and spewing fire through his eyes.

"And you hold no credit to save you from this disaster."

"I don't feel a pinch of remorse for chucking you out of here."

"Enough of rhetoric. Just throw him out of here."

The risk management team didn't hesitate a moment before recommending my termination, and I have nothing to argue with. When I stepped out of the conference room, I glanced at my wristwatch. I was not done with one jolt for the day. I had missed the dinner date with my beautiful Susan. I was late by 30 minutes. When I looked at my phone, I was terrified to find twelve missed calls during that time and a message. I didn't have the courage to call back as I knew her explosive mood. I opened the message which read – *GET LOST*

I had waited upon her on multiple occasions for hours together, but I never resented. I sometimes wondered if it's a girl's prerogative to keep the boy waiting, but a crime otherwise.

I again wondered what I should be worried about now – whether the job or my love. You can earn a job easily, but not love.

I gathered all my courage and dialled her number, but she rejected my call. All my calls faced the same fate, and I knew they would. The safest thing was to send an apology message. I actually mentally thanked her for not picking up my call as I didn't have the courage to deal with her rage.

"Sorry, sweetheart, for breaking your little heart. I feel like a criminal for missing our dinner date. I don't want to bother you with bad news, but I think you should know."

I hesitated a little as I didn't want to share my sorrow and spoil her day. Joy is all I wanted to give her. But I knew that she would not forgive me if I don't share it with her. After all, she swore to share joy and sorrow equally. After much quandary, I decided to text her.

"I lost my job."

I'm sure it will break her heart. But she had to know. There was no response from her. I looked at my watch, which joined hands at 11. She must have slept. I too slept, hoping that the next day would be better. What tomorrow holds for you is always a mystery, a never-ending mystery.

The next morning, I checked for the messages and rightly found a message from my sweetheart.

"Just move on."

I was glad that she wasn't affected much by the loss of my job. I felt proud of her.

"Thank you for understanding. Don't worry, I'll get a job soon."

"I didn't mean your job," was the response I received after a few minutes.

I was dazed by the shock. Was she annoyed that I missed the date? How can she break up for such a reason? Maybe it's a temporary opinion. I should have been more responsible. I decided to meet her and apologise. I knew the best place to meet her was the KFC in her office complex. Since I was jobless, I didn't have to squeeze through my schedule. I arrived at the spot quite early. It was such a cosy place for people to meet. I ordered a mini bucket chicken and started munching just to kill time. Just as I looked around, to my surprise, I saw her walking into the food zone. I knew her work didn't end so soon, but I was glad I wouldn't have to wait longer. As I looked at her with a smile, my smile faded in an instant. I saw a man in his late thirties rush behind her and playfully pinch above her hip. If that surprised me, her response killed me. She laughed gleefully and gave him a mock punch. There was something beyond friendship in their jovial bonding. I hated to believe that. I knew she was a very social person, and she was only being friendly with a colleague. My mind was accusing and defending her at the same time. At one point, I was angry with myself for being such a fool, and at the other, I was ashamed of being suspicious. Maybe the loss of job was playing tricks on my mind. I wanted to talk to her and get it clarified. I didn't have to go to her as she was walking towards me. She was laughing and giggling like a wanton seductress. The couple sat a few metres away from me. They seemed oblivious to the world around them. Staring into each other's eyes, they held their hands as if they were born to be together. I was sitting just in the line of her sight, but she still didn't notice me. Her behaviour was tearing me into shreds. Just as I was staring at her, I saw her expression change. I understood that she came out of the spell and noticed me. The change of expression didn't show regret, but disgust on her face. I felt like jumping off the building. She then returned to a romantic mood and stared back into his eyes, holding his hand, intertwining her fingers with his. She didn't exhibit an iota of discomfort. I was just like one among the many spectators who were witnessing their public display of romance.

'What should I do now? Should I barge in and create a scene? Or should I walk out?'

I didn't think that she was scared of my intrusion. It would only make me look like a loser. I had a feeling that she was observing my quandary. I also had a feeling that she was relishing my plight. At that moment, I knew that walking out without a fuss was the best thing I could do at that time. As I walked to the glass door, I saw her in the reflection on the glass door. Her expression said that she was glad that she got rid of me.

I drank the whole night, but alcohol only aggravated my mental injury. I didn't have any friend so close that I can share my problems. The night didn't seem to end. I kept on drinking till I ran out of stock. I laid down on the floor, crying at the pitch of my voice. The cruel look on her face filled my eyes and tore my heart.

I didn't know when I fell asleep, but when I opened my eyes, there was a mess around. The empty liquor bottles and the leftover side dish scattered around. I was lying on the cold floor like a vagrant. I didn't have to wake up early as I didn't have a job. I didn't have to get myself neat, as I no longer had a girlfriend to care for. In fact, I didn't have to live any longer, as I had no one to live for. As I gradually gained consciousness, I started to feel the coldness of the floor. The thoughts that ran in my mind made me shiver more. I picked up my jacket and rambled out of the house. Every part of my body was working on its own. My eyes were looking somewhere which my mind didn't register, but thinking something, and my legs walked as if they had a brain of their own. I didn't know where I sat and when I got there. I was absolutely dazed, not with alcohol, but with the memories of the previous day's happenings.

❧❦

The continual honking of the trains reminded me of my impending journey – My final journey, a journey of no return.

I stood up and looked around to have one final look at the place. I then started to walk along the railway platform, gazing at the shuffling trains. I was scared a bit, but my motivation was strong enough to beat the fear. As I approached the old man whom I helped a little while ago, he joined his hands in pranam and bowed his head. The tears in his eyes showed how grateful he was. The burden in my heart seemed to have been blown away with the smile of the old man. I was very proud that I was the reason for someone's smile, with whom I was in no way related. I returned a smile and started walking. He stood on his weak, quivering legs, looking in my direction. I involuntarily walked towards him. He held my hands with his frail hands.

"Long live my son. May your life be filled with love and happiness," he blessed me in a feeble voice.

Even though I thought that the blessing of the old man was a stark contradiction to my reality, I felt so happy. I never before knew that making others happy could make us so happy. I held his hand in assurance and continued my walk towards my destiny. I walked beyond the railway platform and further onto the gravel floor along the tracks. After I walked some distance, I picked a track and sat on a concrete slab beside it.

The pounding of the rails under the heavy trains reverberated a long way in a scary echo. As I traced my eyes along my chosen track, I sighted an express train moving towards me, gradually gaining momentum. As the train approached me, I closed my eyes in a silent prayer. Just then, I felt my body tremble. I immediately opened my eyes in horror to find the train still at a couple of hundred metres. I realised that it was my phone. I was not interested in speaking to anyone. But again, I thought that I may not get a chance to speak to anyone anymore. Hence, I picked up the call, which was from an unknown number.

"Hello?" I shouted.

"Hey, hi," I heard a soft voice utter timidly.

When she continued to speak, the train started to honk, a symbolic invitation to my final destination. It took me a long time to gather enough courage to make the decision. I did not want to miss this opportunity, so I thought I had to act quickly.

"I'm busy right now."

"Please don't hang up. I won't take more than a minute. Actually, it took me a long time to gather my courage to make this call. I plead with you to spare me a minute."

I knew that I can't deny the request, not because of the persistence of the girl, but my own curiosity.

"Please go on," I said, but the train, by that time, was thundering towards me, and I was not able to hear her talk. I then started to walk as far from the track as possible. I stopped when the noise subsided.

"Now tell me."

"Look, I know this is a strange conversation, but I felt I had to do it. I'll finish what I have to say. You shall message me your response."

I didn't understand what she was saying.

"I was the girl who sat beside you at the railway platform some time ago. You don't know me, and I don't know much about you. But, the little of what I know about you told me a lot. I appreciate your caring gesture to the old man. I must admit that it was love at first sight. But I can't propose to you looking into your eyes. That's why I got your number so that I can talk to you. I feel so nervous. I don't know if you are married. I don't know if you are committed. I don't know if you will love me despite all this. But I wanted to speak to you as soon as possible as my heart couldn't hold it for long. I love you," she said and disconnected the call in just as much rush as she spoke her words.

I then observed that I had walked quite far from the tracks. I was in a dilemma now. She had just spoken her heart out in a rush and was now waiting for my response. I don't know how to judge her. I recalled what she had spoken. I gained confidence when I realised that she was impressed by my kindness and love for that old man. She proposed to me because she thought that I had a loving heart. When someone values love, they are definitely worthy to be loved.

"I'm neither married nor committed. But I would like to look into your eyes when I reply to your proposal," I messaged her.

Just as I saw the message delivered, I again remembered the old man's words.

"Long live my son. May your life be filled with love and happiness."

When I met her the following day, I looked into her eyes and knew that she was the true love of my life.

It had been 5 years since the day I met her, and my life had been filled with love and happiness, just like the old man blessed.

"You seem to be lost in thoughts, Akash," she said as she walked to me with two cups of coffee, bringing me out of my deep thoughts.

"Hmm, Ya. He is an irresponsible fool," I reiterated her opinion.

I wondered what she would feel like if she knew that I would have done the same, had she not met me. The secret I bore in my heart was a constant burden for me. I was afraid of what she would think of me. I reached for her hand and gave a gentle squeeze.

"I have a confession to make," I said.

She waited for me to speak. She listened to me, jaw-dropped. She had tears when she heard me completely. She held my hand tightly and wept hard. She got up from her seat and hugged me tightly.

"I wanted to meet the old man and thank him for being the reason for all the love we have shared in the years so far and a lot more hereafter. I thank you for considering me a reason to live. I thank God for giving me you." She leaned on my shoulder and wept until my shirt got wet.

As I hugged her tightly, I too wept with her.

Married Strangers

The wedding reception was beautiful, focusing on the grandeur of the stage and the florid walls. The sky was filled with colourful fireworks. The guests were served with mouth-watering delicacies. Stage was set with foot tapping music beats. She walked down the aisle like a beautiful angel, but her face was devoid of a smile. Was she nervous? I liked to believe so, so I did. My eyes saw what I wanted to see. The laughter, the glitter, the buzz made my day very beautiful. Her parents were happy to see their daughter married into a respectable and loving family. She sat beside me in the rear seat of the car, staring out of the window. No words were spoken.

"You look so beautiful in the maroon *gagra*. The credit doesn't go to your dress, anyway," I smiled. She didn't even care to turn towards me in acknowledgement.

I would look at her and attempt to speak, but she wouldn't turn towards me. I thought she was shy. I repeated this a number of times, and that's when I noticed the look in her eyes. She was staring at nothingness, lost in deep thought. It didn't look like thoughts about our happy future. Something was not right. My curiosity started to turn into anxiety. I did not make any attempts to talk to her. I was lost in my own thoughts too. This was not a perfect picture of a newly married couple; both of us turning away from each other and staring outside the window.

Marriage is a social bond, but there was nothing social between the couple. I chose a Porsche two-bedroom seaside apartment to set my family. We were a family of two but occupied both the bedrooms. You might be wondering why the story is running completely on narration. The fact is, there are very few dialogues between the two of us. And it was I who always spoke, only I. I didn't even know how her voice would be. I never heard her utter a single word. There was definitely something wrong. But I did not want to wait until my partner came up with it, unlike the other couples who destroy their relationship with hesitation to take the first step.

"Anu, can I have a word with you?"

"My name is Anupama," she responded sharply.

That's right. I was never so close to her that I can use her short name, although I was married to her. I was not annoyed with her, but definitely discouraged by her approach.

"Yes, Anupama. We are married and a couple now. I see a broad line between us. I mean, do we need to live like strangers in the same house? Do we need to occupy two different bedrooms?"

"You want me to fulfil your sex cravings? Why don't you find someone who could quench your thirst? I'm sure there are plenty, and you have a lot of money."

Her words stabbed me like a knife. As a psychiatrist, I had encountered a lot of repulsive characters, but this was a new experience for me. My experience taught me that every emotion has a deeper bearing, and extreme emotions are mostly a fortress around a vulnerable core. Response in the same terms only aggravates the rift. I took a silent, deep breath.

"Marriage is not an affair, but a bond between two souls. A very special bond. Sex is just a physical obligation, but love is the spiritual bond that makes the relationship very special."

"Thank you for the lecture. I'm not interested."

She walked away dismissively. My effort was shrugged off without any merit.

She never cared what I wanted. She never cared when I left for work or when I returned. She would not even acknowledge my presence. It was like two strangers sharing an apartment, or even worse. I would usually find her talking over the phone, laughing, and giggling. I never knew she could smile.

Is she hostile only towards me? If so, what have I done to deserve that? Is it her nature to be isolated? If so, who is it with whom she was merrily laughing?

I am not suspecting her, just analysing the situation. Sometimes I found that she won't be at home, and I would not know when she would return. Some days she stayed out overnight. I would not be sure if I should look out for her return as I won't know if she would stay out or come home. Her indifference has become a mundane experience for me. But I knew I can't live like this forever. I started staying longer at work. Each day, I started losing hope that the situation would change. My colleagues started to know about my state and felt sorry for me. Some pitied my state, and some mocked me that I was unable to deal with a simple issue.

"Just get rid of her. Get a divorce." advised a close friend of mine.

"I don't think that's the solution to the problem."

"You don't need to solve it, just get rid of it. You don't owe her a thing. She gave you nothing."

"In love, you don't expect to get something, to give."

"What? Love! Yours was an arranged marriage. Someone chose her for you, remember."

"I remember, my friend. I also didn't choose my mother, but I love her. I didn't choose my father, and I love him. So, what if I didn't choose my wife, I love her too."

"Yes, I love her."

"Can love be one-sided? Can you love someone who hates you? Loving someone who hates you is okay, but is it okay to bind them with unrequited love? Is she in love with someone else? Is that why she hates me? Should I give it a pass and move on?"

Questions started to hover around my mind.

Loving someone who hates you is fine. But living with someone who does not like to live with you is not fine.

I gave a deep sigh and made a decision that I believed was good for both of us. I could not decide what she wanted without consulting with her. Again, it's the most uncomfortable part of the plan.

"I gotta do what I gotta do."

I made up my mind and went home early that day. She was not there in the house. I wasn't sure if I should call it a home. It was just a building made of bricks and mortar, sheltering two indifferent individuals. I sat in my recliner, with my eager eyes fixed at the door, but my mind wandering along the roads leading to an uncertain future, reminding me of my matrimonial oath that the journey would be accompanied by my life partner till the end. I was prepared to break that oath, to fulfil another one. Yes… Didn't I also promise to fulfil her wishes and keep her happy? I was so captivated in my thoughts that I did not keep track of time, until the clock alerted me with a gentle stroke. I was counting it as I kept my gaze fixed at the door. The clock calmed down after striking twelve times. I had been waiting for around three hours, but to no avail. I finally came to a conclusion that she wouldn't return for the day. I decided to sleep in the hall that night. I succumbed to yet another sleepless night with mixed feelings; half happy that the annoying discussion didn't happen, half anxious about her safety. It was a longer night comparatively. I didn't know when I slept, but I was woken by a distant sound of a phone ringing. Sleepily, I reached for my phone, but the dark screen suggested that it was not the culprit. The ringing still continued. I rubbed my eyes and trailed the source of the sound to Anupama's room. The time was 8 AM.

"Didn't know what time she came last night."

I stretched my arms and yawned lazily.

I was glad that she came back, but worried that the discussion would take place. I observed that the phone didn't stop ringing. I understood that she was still asleep, so I decided to wait until she woke up. As I laid down on the recliner in the hall, I dozed off.

The phone rang again. I was sleeping outside the closed room, and yet the sound of the phone ringing disturbed my sleep. How could she sleep despite the constant disturbance from within the same room?

"Maybe she is tired," I thought.

But something was scary to me. The ringing of the phone reverberated within the walls in an ominous echo.

"Is she not well? Did something terrible happen? Why won't she silence the phone if she's not going to pick it up?"

Multiple thoughts bombarded my mind. I was not able to come to a conclusion.

"Should I barge in? Should I knock her door? Should I just wait?"

The phone kept ringing and ringing. I made up my mind and walked to her door. I gently knocked on the door.

"Anu… Anupama. Anupama," I hesitantly called out.

I then knocked on the door harder. As my attempts failed, fear crept within. I decided to break in. My hands shivered. I banged onto the door with my shoulder. It didn't work out like it does in the movies. I pulled the dining table and glided it against the door. Since the floor was made of marble tiles, the table glided smoothly and made the necessary impact on the door. As I sustained my efforts to break open the door, my legs shivered with wild imagination of finding her unconscious on the floor, drenched in a pool of blood.

"You should have brought her a little earlier, we would have saved her."

The routine dialogue of a film doctor scared me of unbearable consequences.

"Maybe I should have thought about this a little earlier."

I gathered more power and banged the door with full force. The door opened with a thud. I almost fell forward after the table. Without wasting a second, I rushed into her bedroom. This is the first time I was stepping into her bedroom since the day she stepped into the house. She had maintained her bedroom quite tastefully. For an instant, I forgot the purpose of breaking into her bedroom. Suddenly, I started to panic. She was not on her bed. Maybe she fell on the other side. I rushed to the other side of the bed. She was not there too.

My heart started to beat faster. I looked around in horror. My sight caught the bathroom door. I slowly walked towards the bathroom door. It was hard to even swallow my saliva. My throat was choked. I slowly held the knob of the bathroom door and turned it slowly. It was unlocked. My mind flashed the images of her unconscious body on the bathroom floor, blood stream running through her slit wrist. As the door opened, my eyeballs popped out of my sockets. I started sweating profusely, and my legs trembled in horror. The sight in front of me was more frightening than my imagination. I slowly and anxiously walked into the bathroom, carefully inspecting the spine-chilling spectacle.

I stared at myself in the mirror, which reflected my face, pale in horror. The writing across my face on the mirror was in blood-red. For a second, I suspected it was blood, but then upon close examination, found it was her lipstick. However, what was written was more serious than what it was written with.

Life didn't offer anything worth living for. Hence, I'm ending my life. My decision to end my life is purely based on my own disinterest in life. Nobody holds responsibility for my decision.

The words on the mirror rang in my mind like a fire alarm. I squatted on the bathroom floor and sat frozen. My mind was clouded, and my thoughts ran against a wall. I didn't know what to do. I still heard the phone ringing. Immediately, I crept towards her bedside table and picked up the phone.

I was not sure if I should pick up the phone. I was not sure what I would be hearing on the call. I was not sure of anything. I attended the call with shivering fingers. The tone on the other side didn't offer respite to my mental turmoil.

"Are you Anu's husband?" asked the voice on the other end.

"Yes, I am," I said, anxiously waiting for the message.

"Can you please immediately come to the Nanavati Hospital?"

Now, my fear started to turn real.

"Wh… What? Why?" I stammered.

"Come soon," the voice said and hung up the call.

༄༅

"Why did you do this?" I asked Anupama, who was in a wheelchair, bandaged on her forehead and arms. She got drunk and crashed her car against the over-bridge pillar at full speed. She miraculously survived.

"I don't like this marriage," she bluntly said.

"Then, why did you marry?"

"Do I have the freedom to decide?"

"Are you in love with someone?"

"No."

"Then, don't you like me?"

"I didn't like the way I was pushed for a marriage. You see the girl at some function; you lose your heart and choose the girl for marriage as if you choose a doll from a shop. You never care about the girl. All you care about is yourselves," she screamed and sobbed.

I listened to her patiently and let her finish.

"You know what? I saw you for the first time at our wedding."

Anupama stopped sobbing and stared at me in surprise.

"You heard it right. I was so busy with my profession that I never had the chance to fall in love with anyone. When my parents decided to get me married, I didn't refuse. I let them choose a girl for me, and I agreed to the marriage only after your family replied that you were happy with the relationship. I knew that I'd love you with all my heart and confident that my love would be reciprocated."

"You cannot plan or arrange love. Remember, we had an arranged marriage."

"But it's a marriage. It's a special bond, and I respect that. Love is imminent in marriage."

"Love can't happen forcefully."

"If you can't love me, you can get a divorce. Although I'm against the idea of divorce, I believe life is more valuable."

"I can't live to disappoint my parents with that idea."

"I respect your feelings. Let's make a deal. We can live in the same house, respecting our boundaries, and lead our own lives."

"Can I ask you a question?" she asked thoughtfully.

"Sure."

"You could have seen me before the wedding day. Why didn't you?"

"Because I don't like to select my life partner like furniture from the catalogue."

She looked straight into his eyes with some newfound respect.

"We may not be a couple, but we don't need to be strangers either. I can be your friend if you accept. I promise you, I'll be a good friend." I promised

"Friends…?" I said, offering my hand to her.

She gave a mild smile and tried to shake my hand, but winced in pain as she suffered multiple fractures.

"It's okay. Relax, Anupama."

"Anu, call me Anu," she said as she looked into my eyes.

We had a different perspective of each other. It was the start of a new phase in our lives. I hope that our friendship could be a foundation for a special bond. Keeping trust in the future, I started the new journey with her.

Unconditional Love

She walked down the aisle, adorned in a white flowing wedding gown, with a netted veil that partially covered her face. With a stoic expression, she refused to reveal her inner feelings. No one knows if she was happy or sad, tense or excited.

Michael, do you take Diana to be your wedded wife, to live together in marriage? Do you promise to love her, comfort her, honour and keep her, for better or worse, for richer or poorer, in sickness and health, and forsaking all others, be faithful only to her, for as long as you both shall live?

I do.

Diana, do you take Michael to be your wedded husband to live together in marriage? Do you promise to love him, comfort him, honour and keep him, for better or worse, for richer or poorer, in sickness and in health, and forsaking all others, be faithful only to him so long as you both shall live?

I do.

I sprang up from my bed in the midnight, breathless. I was trying to sleep, but the wedding oath kept playing and replaying in my mind. We were in love for five years and vowed to never part. She vowed the same last week, but the one holding her hand was someone else.

"How can she do this to me? How can she break her promise to me and hold someone else's hand? I hate her. I HATE HER."

I switched on the lights and walked towards the balcony. As I walked to the balcony, I swept my glance across the walls of my bedroom, which had handwritten notes all over the walls – "*I hate you, Diana.*"

But that didn't help much, as the walls of my heart had so firmly written I love you, Diana.

Hating someone you love is more difficult than loving someone you hate.

Does it apply to her? If she loves me, why did she marry someone else? If I'm suffering in pain, how can she live in peace? Cheating in love is a crime worse than murder because it kills you every moment of your life.

I was wandering along my balcony, sleeplessly, and I wondered what she would have been doing now. When it occurred to me that she would be snuggling in a thick blanket with her husband in a tight hug, I regretted thinking about it.

It's chill weather outside, and I'm loitering on my balcony, which has a sea-facing view, wearing only my boxers and a vest. A weather that would have been embraced as a blessing has turned into a nightmare. The gentle sound of the waves hitting the shore and the silvery moon that shone through the translucent clouds would have stirred my heart with romantic exuberance, but no more did. I tried a lot to forget her. When I was not able to forget her, I tried to hate her. All the pain was because I still loved her. I wanted to stop loving her. But the problem was that you cannot choose whether to love or not because love is not what you do; it happens. And when it happens, it stays forever.

I heard people drink when they fail in love to get rid of the painful memories. But I didn't understand how alcohol could defeat an emotion so strong that is etched at the depth of your heart. I didn't believe in alcohol.

Time rushed so fast that I sometimes kept wondering how things went wayward.

∽

I was popular among girls in the college. Dance and music were my passion. I was always in the spotlight during the college cultural events and inter-college music competitions. I had quite a few proposals from the girls of my college and also other colleges. When it comes to the relationship of hearts, you seek something in the person you love that you wouldn't be able to explain. The same was the case with me. None of the girls invoked that feeling in me until the day she walked to me with that luminous smile that brightened my life for a few years. We shared the same opinions and had the same likes most often. We were like born for each other.

We graduated from college together. I gathered a group of enthusiasts and formed a music band. She was interested in pursuing higher studies abroad. Though I hated to part with her, I convinced myself that the separation would allow us to focus on our careers. I also heard that separation strengthens the bond of hearts. That was just a consolation. I saw her off at the airport to let her pursue her post-graduation. We promised to keep in touch, and I gave her a farewell kiss.

The band started to work on composing music albums. We were not successful in our attempts. Every time we worked on an album, we felt that it was going to sway the world, but it would be rejected outright. Our confidence was knocked down every time. But we stood up again, though not with the same vigour. In the continual efforts striving to succeed in our career, I was not able to respond to her calls and messages. The world was not kind to unestablished artists like us. The spirits of the band went down. We even lost a couple of guys in the endeavour. Finding replacements for them was a huge task.

Finally, one medium-range production company had agreed to make an album with our band. I was so elated that my heart automatically took my thoughts to Diana. The struggle for success and identity has sucked all my time and energy that I didn't notice two years had flown away without notice. She had even completed her post-graduation and returned to India. I was so excited that I wanted to share the joy of success with her. My heart was beating faster. It was a dream come true for me. The phone rang for a long time. Just as I thought that she wouldn't pick the call, I heard the click of the phone.

"Hello, my Diana." I shouted in excitement.

"Hello." she replied.

"You won't know how glad I am. You know…"

"Where have you been all these days, Daniel?"

"Daniel? Not Dan?" I thought.

"Building a beautiful world for us: You and me."

"You took a very long time."

"Yes, baby. It's quite long, but…"

"I mean, it's too late, Daniel."

What did she mean?

I was not sure if I had heard it right.

"Do you know how many times I tried to reach you? How many days I have cried in my silent, lonely nights? You were never there when I needed you."

"You know, I was working on building a career."

"Your career is more important to you than me. There can't be a relationship when there is no love."

"I was working on building a future: a better future for both of us, damn it."

"There is no more 'us', Daniel." she said without much effort.

"What do you mean?"

"I'm getting engaged to my colleague from post-graduation. He loves me a lot."

I didn't hear anything after that. I was not sure if she spoke after that or disconnected the call. My mind was crowded with questions. The first question was whether I was dreaming. I checked my phone to see if the call really happened. It was not a dream. Was it a joke? It didn't look so.

I wanted to talk to her, but I didn't try to call her because she left no scope for discussion. Then again, the questions didn't cease to pour.

Is she subjected to any pressure? Is she forced into a marriage against her will?

A forlorn heart seeks hope in hopelessness.

I was not sure if I was invited or not, but I decided to go to her wedding. Just to check if she was wilfully getting married to someone else. When I saw her walk down the aisle, the first thing I did was to look at her face for expressions. She didn't look happy. Perhaps that's what I wanted to believe. Despite all my efforts, I couldn't deny the fact that she wore a smile on her partially veiled face. I couldn't tell if she saw me amongst the crowd. But my heart told me that she saw me, and she didn't have a trace of remorse.

A scorned heart sees darkness, even in the sun.

When she can happily move on with her life, why can't I? Moving on is not a bad move. It really worked well for me, though it was a little difficult. I began to focus on life and career. I wondered how time has erased my pain. Time is the greatest healer. But there is something that time can't do: Erase her memories.

I moved on with my life. My first music album was a huge success. *Life is not unfair after all. It's just a mixed package.* It did hold me a lot of pleasant surprises. I started to lead a successful and happy life. Bigger production companies started to swarm us, but we stayed with the first company. They also grew in stature with our success. I did date a couple of girls, but none appealed to me as Diana did. But I knew that life would be holding yet another good surprise for me.

Years passed, and my life came to normalcy. I got over my failed relationship, but life always comes full circle. Once, when I was returning from a concert, I saw a fuming car on the sideway. I slowed down and approached the car. I saw a lady kicking the wheel in frustration. I stopped my car and walked towards her.

"May I help you?" I offered help.

When she turned to face me, my heart skipped a beat.

"Diana!"

She stared at me with an uncomfortable smile.

"You left me at the crossroads of my life, broke. Here you are now. Why should I help you?" This thought occurred to me on an impulse.

"Can I help you?"

She stared at me in disbelief.

"I quit on you when you needed me the most. I chose to lead a comfortable life without supporting you. Aren't you annoyed with me?"

Despite all my efforts, I was not able to hate her.

"I wouldn't blame you. Any girl would have done the same. A girl needs love more than anything, which I didn't give you. Mistake was mine. You did right. I would be glad to know that you are happy with your life now."

She was in tears.

"Yes, I'm happy. My husband loves me a lot. I have a son who is three years old now. I have a beautiful family."

I was really happy to know that she's happy.

"We may not be lovers, but I guess that doesn't stop us from being good friends." I extended my hand to her. She held my hand and shook it happily.

I may have lost the love of my life, but I earned a good friend.

I have always wondered about scorned lovers who hold a lifetime grudge with their ex. How can you hate someone you loved so much? Does love have a validity period? Is love conditional?

Life is an uncertain ride with ups and downs, rise and fall, joy and pain, gifts and curses. But love is a certain experience that sustains all. Holding a grudge against your ex is insulting your love.

Ticket Please

It was the first day of my college, and I need not mention how excited I am. College life is always a realisation of a long-awaited dream for any school kid. Ever since my 12th board exams got completed, I was ecstatic in every process of my college endeavour, from debating on the course I was going to do, the college I chose to pursue my graduation, getting the application forms, etc. Finally, I got my admission in Loyola College for Visual Communications. I chose the college because it was well-known for fun activities from cultural to sports. Also, the college was a premise for innumerable hit movies. Many notable and celebrated movie stars, sports stars, politicians, and spiritual leaders were alumni of this great college. I felt like I was going to join some elite club that I couldn't wait to step into the college. On my persuasion, some of my school friends did post their applications to join the college, but unfortunately, I was the only one from my group to have got the admission. As a school child, I always dreamt of being a part of one of the merry college groups, who do a lot of fun and noise on the bus. Since this was my first day in college, I had to settle for a solo ride. The MTC bus was still in the stand while the morning rays of the sun pierced through the window glass and caressed my face. You can never be a fan of the Chennai sun, but everything seemed beautiful today. When your heart is filled with joy, the world around you is always beautiful. I inhaled the fresh morning breeze which would shortly be polluted with smoke and dust. The crowd started to slowly occupy the empty seats. I always block the seat beside me until the last seat in the bus is filled, hoping that some of my friends might accidentally happen to travel on the same bus. With the force of habit, I placed my bag on the seat beside me while I glanced out of the window with a hope of finding some company.

"Is the seat occupied?"

The rude voice drew my attention. As I turned around, I saw a middle-aged man with a grumpy face. Half-heartedly, I yanked my bag out of the seat. He occupied the seat without any acknowledgement. The sun now gradually started scorching my face. All the seats in the bus are now occupied, and the crowd started to fill the empty space in the bus on their foot. By rule, the MTC bus is considered empty until there is any space that could fit two more feet. The conductor is skilful enough to pierce through the crowd and tender tickets.

The man beside me should be more than 120 kilograms, as he also occupied part of my seat. Early this morning, he stunk like he had toiled all day with garbage. I wondered when was the last time he took a bath. I no longer enjoyed the ride. As he shuffled uncomfortably in his seat, he gazed at me as if I had occupied his part of the seat. Avoiding his gaze, I looked outside, cursing my rotten luck. I shuddered at the thought of travelling over an hour with this suffocating discomfort. The fresh morning breeze is already contaminated by his stench. Resigning to my fate, I stared outside without any interest. But my eyes sparkled at a beautiful sight. A girl who looked like a college-going student, in a white printed top and faded denim jean, gaited on her three-inch white multi-strap stilettos. Her dense black curly hair bounced in rhythm, and her silver string earrings matched the tune as if they were dancing to a song. Although she breezed away like a dream, her image lingered in my eyes as if she was framed in my retina.

"Ticket." I heard the authoritative voice of the bus conductor, who was impatient of my dreamy reverie. I fumbled with my wallet as I was guilty of wasting the conductor's time, who was dealing with an unconcerned crowd. I was careful in giving the exact fare as I knew that he was already annoyed with me. As he passed me, I breathed a sigh of relief, but the sight of my unpleasant co-passenger reminded me of my pathetic condition. Once again, I turned towards the window and started peeking outside, just as the engine whirred into life. I heard the conductor shouting at a passenger.

"Can't you bring the right change? Why can't you rich people find a more suitable ride?"

I mentally agreed with the conductor. *"When you know that you are going to need the change, why can't you begin it with you, careless punk?"* I thought.

I turned back to the conductor, whose seat was just behind me, to see who the offender was. I saw a slender hand holding a five hundred rupees note. The familiar face that had enticed me a few moments earlier appeared again. Her image gradually came into sight as she slowly ascended the stairs.

"How can you expect everyone to have change, moron?" I thought as I suddenly felt the conductor was wrong.

He snatched the money and scribbled something on the back of the ticket.

"Get your change later," he barked.

I saw the person grab the ticket and tried to squeeze past the crowd to the centre of the bus, but the crowd was immense. Hence, she stopped her attempts, and I thanked her for that because she was now standing just adjacent to me. But she didn't give up her attempts easily. When she understood that her efforts were in vain, she resigned to her fate and got settled where she stood. In the pretext of watching outside, I saw her in the reflection of the window glass. I now started to hate my co-passenger more. I was even afraid she might move away, unable to bear his stench. I wished someone would throw him out as he was spoiling the beautiful atmosphere of the bus. Out of the blue, he stood up and slapped his forehead with his palm. "Not again." he mumbled as he rushed out of the bus, scattering everyone off his path. The girl quickly occupied the vacant seat. My heart started beating louder. For a moment, I was afraid someone would precede her. My lips instantly curved into a smile. I was happy for two reasons. One was that I would no longer need to bear the suffocation of the unbearable stench any longer with the exit of the man beside me. The second was even more happiness. The girl, who I thought was just a passing cloud, is now going to sit beside me and travel a distance. Everything seemed like a miracle to me. The atmosphere again turned beautiful. She calmly sat beside me, shuffled the contents of her handbag, picked out her android phone, and started to play music. Even though I didn't expect anything better than that, I felt a little disappointed. Today was supposed to be my 'miracle day.' I calmly watched her from the reflection of the window glass as she was enjoying her music. Even I was enjoying the music that played in my heart. I then realised that in the movies when the hero falls in love, the song that follows is not a mere figment of cinematic creation after all. When I just looked around, I saw a few young faces smiling at my luck and a few fuming at their bad luck. I felt like I was a winner of some coveted trophy.

Was it love at first sight? Or was it just a joy of beauty? - I did not know. I was just experiencing the bliss. As I was transported to a different world, I didn't know how far we had travelled, but the bus suddenly jerked to a stop. The bus was parked on the roadside for ticket checking. Some extra time in her company. I stole glances at her while she was busy with the music. She looked to be in her late teens. Her face glowed with her flawless skin and vivid facial features. Her bright eyes stared at the mobile screen as her fingers fiddled with something on the screen, and her well-manicured eyelashes looked like a perfect art. Strands of her curled hair occasionally fell on her face, which she playfully blew away with her red lips that looked like a pair of blood-soaked orange carpels. As I was engrossed in her beauty, I almost forgot why the bus was stopped. A group of men in their late forties swarmed the bus from both exits. The ticket checkers' entry was strategic so that defaulters cannot escape them. One of the ticket checkers approached our seat and asked for our tickets. Just as I was about to retrieve mine, I saw her face flushed in panic. She was searching her jeans pockets and handbag, but her expressions said that something was not right. Even I delayed picking mine. The ticket checker, in the meantime, was checking the others' tickets while he still stood at us.

"Any problem?" I spoke my first words after gathering enough courage.

"Mind your business." she said.

I was annoyed at her dismissive attitude, but then again, I understood her state of mind. I knew that she missed her ticket somewhere while she made her way to the seat. Inconspicuously, I picked up my ticket and dropped it at her feet.

"Is that what you are searching for?"

"What?"

"Is that what you are searching for?" I repeated, pointing at the bit of paper at her feet.

She heaved a sigh of relief and picked it.

"Here is my ticket." she handed her ticket to the ticket collector.

"Where is your ticket, mister?"

"Well, you are holding it." I wanted to tell, but I showed him a blank face.

"Get out of your seat." he said.

I saw the bus leaving me with the group of old men while I was having the moment of my life some time ago. It was as if I was left alone on an isolated island, while the ship, which was my only hope, was sailing away in utter disdain. I looked back at the old men who stared at me like hungry wolves. They started making some calculations and scribbled something on their receipt book. He tore the page and handed it to me as if he was writing me a hefty cheque.

"Pay the fine and leave."

"Fine? Why should I pay a fine?" I thought

I looked at the slip which he had handwritten.

"Five hundred?! That much?"

POV - Girl on the bus:

"I do not want to be late for my first day at college." I muttered as I strapped my stilettos in a hurry.

I quickly jumped onto my lemon yellow Vespa and zoomed off on my ever-reliable cutie wheels. As I sped through the sparsely morning traffic, I remembered how much I hated the city. Everything about the city reaffirmed that I do not belong here. I had to leave my hometown, Ludhiana, and my friends and my memories – everything – all because of my father's damn job. He gets transferred on duty, and we follow suit. We do not have a choice. I honked my way through to the bike parking. I do not know the people or the language. Somehow, I managed to get done with the parking formalities and ran to the bus stand. I was apprised of the basic information that I would need. I knew the bus numbers, phone numbers, and some most important words that could sail me through with little help from the strange people. My father often told me that Chennai people are very friendly and helpful in nature. I knew that he was trying to make me feel better. The more he praised, the more I hated the city. Half-heartedly, I waited at the bus station scanning for the bus numbers. The first bus that came into my sight looked full, and I started to look for other buses that ran through my route but were worse than the first one. Hesitantly, I walked back to the first bus, which seemed better, and slowly stepped onto the footboard. Nobody seemed to budge. I had to fight through the crowd to reach the conductor. And when I did, I had another ordeal to deal with.

"Can't you bring the right change? Why can't you rich people find a more suitable ride?"

He snatched the 500 rupee note from my hand and then scribbled something on the back of the ticket.

"Get your change later." he shouted as he stuffed the ticket in my hand.

I wanted to shout back, but I thought better of it and quietly walked through the crowd, studying scribbling at the back side of the ticket. The crowd didn't seem to budge as I tried to squeeze through to the centre where there will be least commotion. I had to stop my attempts as the crowd was impregnable. Within seconds, a pungent smell pierced my nostrils, which almost suffocated me to death. I tried my best to move away, but none from the crowd was willing to take my place. Left with no other options, I stood where I was, cursing my father for bringing me here. Somehow, I felt reprieve when the bulky man who spread the terrible stench jumped off his seat and rushed out of the bus. It was double delight for me. One was that I no longer had to tolerate the suffocating stench, and the other one was that I got a seat. I swiftly occupied the empty seat before anyone. Heaving a sigh of relief, I fished out my android phone and played my favourite music. Music always plays such a soothing effect on me that I forgot all the inconvenience and got immersed in the mesmerising melodies. As I closed my eyes, I was transported back in time to Ludhiana where I spent memorable moments with longtime friends at the Pavilion Mall, where we used to merrily roam all day, window shopping. Memories of my school friends partying at the Biker's Café filled my heart with inexplicable bliss, and endless gossiping at Mustafa Chacha's chai shop flashed in my mind like a cinema scope. As the memories captivated my mind, I didn't realise how far I had travelled but was yanked out of my reverie when the bus came to a sudden halt. As I opened my eyes, I saw that the bus was parked on the roadside in the shade of a huge tree. Everything happening around her is adding to her repulsive mindset. There was some uneasy commotion in the bus. When I looked around, I saw a group of middle-aged men strategically horde the bus from both ends. I ignored the commotion and focused back into my music. But it was not long before one of the old wolves approached my seat.

"Show me your ticket." shouted the man, startling me.

I switched off the music and checked my pockets for the ticket, but was shocked that I didn't find it. As I checked my pockets in panic, he gave me a suspicious look, which embarrassed me. The ticket was nowhere to be found.

"More misfortune." I cursed my fate.

The ticket checker was checking others' tickets, but he didn't move away from me, as though he was blocking me from an escape.

"Do I need anything more to hate the city?"

"Any problem?" the guy seated beside me asked.

"Mind your business."

"Always willing to help a young girl, the great Samaritans." I thought in frustration as I was busy shuffling the bag, in search of my ticket.

"Is that what you are searching for?"

I understood that he was not the one who gives up easily.

"WHAT?" I shouted.

"Is that what you are searching for?" he said, picking up a piece of paper from the floor.

"Thank God!"

I snatched it from his hand, heaving a sigh of relief.

"Here's my ticket." I shoved it at the ticket checker.

He did a little bit of scrutiny and returned my ticket to me.

"Where is your ticket, mister?" he asked my co-passenger.

He failed to come up with an answer, which suggested that he didn't have one.

"Ticketless travellers! They won't spend a few rupees to buy a ticket, but they are all generous to offer help to a young girl."

I slanted my legs away, offering him some space to walk out of his seat.

"It's not really that bad a day." I thought as I happily glided to the window seat vacated by the ticket defaulter in my sitting position. A girl of my age group took the seat beside me. I was happier with the way things were turning out and felt more comfortable.

"Can you please let me know when the bus approaches Loyola College?" I asked the girl beside me, and the girl beside me nodded with a smile. I continued with my music, which I started enjoying a little better. Shutting my eyes, I relished the music that helped me forget the time.

"Next, is your stop." The girl beside me announced.

I opened my eyes with a start as I was unaware of the time. With a smile of gratitude, I nodded to her as I unplugged the headphones from my mobile and placed them in my handbag in a hurry. As I got up from my seat, I remembered that the conductor was supposed to return the change for my 500 rupees. I quickly walked up to the conductor and gave him the ticket, but he returned a confused look.

"What do you want?" he asked.

"I wanted the change for the 500 rupees that I gave you. You mentioned it at the back of the ticket."

"Where did I mention?" he said, returning my ticket back to me.

"Here…!" I was shocked to find that my finger was pointing to the spotless back of the ticket.

"There must have been some mistake. Don't you remember, I gave you a 500 rupee note?"

"Please, madam. Show me where I have mentioned, and I shall return the change. And now, will you please move. You are blocking the path."

I stepped off the bus at my stop with mixed feelings. Anger, frustration, sadness, and fear played a horrible medley in my messed-up mind.

"It's a cheap trick that the conductor played. He shall pay for his dishonesty." I cursed in my mind and half-heartedly walked into the enormous campus of Loyola College. There were students in batches cracking jokes, playing pranks, and making merry. The classrooms were noisy with excitement. The first day at college was nothing but introductions and icebreakers. It was as if the purpose of college was to know each other and have fun. I could see all happy faces around. Probably, I'm the only one who is sad in the whole campus. I was sad, sad for various reasons. I was sad that the conductor had cheated me of my money; I was sad that my father had to get transferred to this terrible place and I had to bear the punishment for his official consequences, and most of all, I had to miss my childhood friends with whom I shared most of my years. Few of my classmates tried to get familiar with me, but I was preoccupied with my misfortunes that I was not able to reciprocate their spirit. Absent-mindedly, I swivelled my pen between my fingers as I stared straight ahead, but my mind registered nothing. Suddenly, the pen slipped from my hand and fell at my foot. When I bent down to pick up my pen, I found a piece of paper perched at my toe in the stiletto strap. I carefully picked it up, with my mind unable to reason the happening. There was something written on a thin newsprint quality paper. I guess I knew what it was. With my heart beating erratically, I unfolded the piece of paper. There

was no mistaking it. As I stared at the bit of paper, my mind started to analyse the situation.

"Is that what you are searching for?"

Now, I understood what had happened.

"Any problem?"

"Mind your business."

"Oh no! What have I done?"

"Where is your ticket, mister?"

He gave his ticket to me and saved me from embarrassment, despite my rude behaviour.

"Please, madam. Show me where I have mentioned, and I shall return the change."

Of course! Why should he keep track of my balance amount? He should have been giving tickets to many thousands a day. I should have safely produced the ticket to him. It was my mistake.

In an instant, realisation hit me like a lightning bolt. I knew I had been living with a misconception; my co-passenger, the conductor, the people of the city on the whole. All my judgements have gone wrong. And I sincerely regretted that. I wished that I get a chance to go back in time and apologise to them; especially him, my co-passenger. I began to recollect him amid the mental debate. He was a tall, well-built teenager with masculine facial features. He had a square face with a round nose and a prominent dimple that enhanced his smile. With neatly cropped hair and his square face, he looked good enough to be an army soldier, but the dimple on his cheek and innocent smile made him a rare combination of manliness and innocence. His helping tendency and gentle behaviour enhanced his appeal. Church always offered solace when my mental turmoil is beyond my control. I was lucky to have a beautiful church within the campus. I walked to the church through the road laden with green trees on either side. The enormous white edifice with a slender pointed spire that stood 157 foot tall looked like it could pierce the clusters of white clouds that lay scattered in the deep blue sky. I stepped into the huge entrance which was plain and simple, but the divine ambience within calmed my mind and the rows of empty wooden benches added to my peace of mind. With a newfound peace, I walked out of the church. As I strolled along the football court, I saw a group of youngsters who looked to have just finished a game. As I withdrew my sight, something forced me to look back again. There was a guy just about six feet in height, who was packing his bag, but he was facing away from me. I sensed something similar about the person. With bated breath, I waited for him to turn around. After what felt like an eternity, he turned around to leave. My heart started to beat faster when my mind began the recognition program. I also ran a silent prayer, but luck was not on my side. I calmly stepped aside as he walked past me. It was not him.

I realised that I can't have peace of mind until I talk to him. I will find him someday and apologise to him. Maybe he will accept my apology. Maybe he will accept my friendship.

We shall make good friends. As I thought of him as a friend, my heart found an inexplicable solace.

Maybe I blushed. I was not sure.

Would I meet him again? I don't know.

Would he be my friend after my despicable behaviour? I don't know.

The only thing I knew was that I would be looking for him at the bus stand where I met him first. I would be hoping to find him. Maybe he will be my co-passenger once again, and many more times. I wish he would agree to be my friend. I only wish.

Follow Me

"Karthik, wake up! It's half past eight. Get out of your bed and pick up your book. Your semester exams are not too far."

Karthik woke up lazily with the persistent wake-up calls from his mother. He hated his Sunday mornings since his final semester exam schedule was announced. After six days of strenuous lectures, his weekend didn't offer him reprieve.

"God, why do I have to study? Turn me into one of those birds or animals which lead a happy life without having to read." He prayed, but hesitantly took his book and walked to the open window. He leaned forward on the window sill, shutting his eyes, inhaling the late morning breeze. Just as he opened his eyes, a pleasant sight awaited him. A beautiful girl in a knee-length floral bodycon dress gracefully walked the road. Till she disappeared at the end of the road, she captured his sight and then, afterwards, his heart.

'Why didn't I see her all these days?' he wondered, and also if he would see her again. He didn't need a reason to be bored of his books, but he has one now. The whole day, her thoughts kept him entertained.

After a weeklong college torture again, the Sunday somehow instilled enthusiasm. This time, he didn't need his mother's wake-up call. He woke up at seven, much to the surprise of his mother. He finished his morning chores and dutifully got settled at the window with a book that invoked the least interest in him. His mind and heart were on the road, expecting the same girl to feast his eyes. The wait was a torture he had never experienced, mostly because he was not sure if it would be fruitful.

"She was a random girl who crossed my sight. How can I expect to see her again? Why should I be so restless about her?"

The questions taunted him, but he didn't thrive on the questions, just followed his heart.

Finally, his wait came to an end when the same girl appeared on the road in front of his window at around the same time. He stared at her, drooling at her elegance and style. It looked like a one-way affair as the girl didn't care to look away from the road ahead. He was happy in a way that he didn't have to be embarrassed getting caught staring at the girl, as she didn't notice him. But he was also sad that she didn't notice a sincere admirer. Nevertheless, he just enjoyed the short spectacle that filled his whole day with bliss.

Unknowingly, this became his Sunday custom. Every time, he made sure that she didn't see him watching her. But his heart asked for more. Hence, he thought of getting closer to her. He then decided to follow her. The next Sunday was received with immense anticipation. He woke up earlier than his usual days and took a long bath. He picked his best dress and got ready to execute his plan, yet he was not so determined. When he saw her at the far end of the road, he quickly rushed to his door. As he saw her approach his house, he turned hesitant. He gathered all his courage and stepped out as she crossed his house. Cautiously, he followed her at a safe distance, afraid of being caught stalking a girl. Thankfully, she didn't look back. After a short walk, he saw her open the shutters of a book store. He quickly walked past the store and disappeared at the next turn of the road. He was glad he was successful in finding her destination.

"What next?" he thought, as he didn't have the guts to approach a girl and confess his liking for her.

He went back home wondering what his next step would be. The only idea that occurred to him was to meet her under the pretext of purchasing a book. Though it sounded like a cliché, it didn't seem to be a bad idea. He didn't take long to implement his plan. Quietly, he walked into the sparsely crowded bookstore, glancing at her from the corner of his eye. She was at the billing counter, finalising a sale with a customer. Aimlessly, he wandered along the bookshelves, seizing every opportunity to catch a glimpse of her. Unaware that he was browsing through the modest shelves longer than necessary, he saw her notice him. When he noticed her walking towards him, he panicked, fumbling with the books on the shelf.

"Can I help you?" she asked.

He gave a sigh of relief, but he was at a loss of ideas.

"I… I have been looking for…"

"I mean, I want to check if you have application mechanics. I mean, applied mechanics." he stuttered.

She gave him a customary smile.

"Please let me help you with it." she said, and right away went for the appropriate shelf and picked the book in a couple of seconds.

"Anything else you are looking for?"

"No."

"Please follow me."

"That's what I have been doing all these days," he thought naughtily.

She walked him to the billing counter.

"Please give me a minute." she said, working on the computer.

He occasionally stole glances at her. She looked at him for a few seconds as he deliberately looked away from her. She took a couple of minutes before she placed the book in front of him and kept the bill in the book.

"Three hundred rupees for the book." she said.

He paid the money and took the book.

"Please do visit us again." she said with a smile.

He left the bookstore without looking back, wondering if she really meant to visit again. It didn't matter to him.

He continued his visits to the bookshop every Sunday but maintained nonchalance. She greeted him with a smile every time he visited the bookshop, but he couldn't gather the courage to speak up his heart. One Sunday when he visited the bookshop, the usual smile was missing. He wondered if his intentions were exposed as he didn't miss a weekend. He bought some random book that fell into his hands, which could have raised suspicion. When he was settling the bill, she didn't give her usual smile. He felt nervous and left immediately. He didn't see her walk the road the following Sunday. He thought he might have missed her, though he had never missed her on any day. He hurried to the bookshop to find an old man sitting at the counter. He didn't know how to ask for her. He thought that she might have had some other commitment. With that thought, he visited the bookshop the next week, but she was still not there. He never again found her walk that road or in the bookshop. He felt so sad but consoled himself that it was a short phase of his life that will be cherished forever.

Five years later, he almost got over his first love that never took off. Nevertheless, it was his first love. He got settled in a high-profile job in a prestigious company and shifted to a new city, but her memories stayed with him. His parents started looking for a bride for him. He was never interested in looking at the proposals, but he secretly wished if one of the proposals could have her photo. It was a long shot, though. Once his cousin sister visited him for holidays. After they had a short chat, when she was roaming in the house, she caught sight of the crazy collection of books. It surprised her as she knew that her cousin was not a voracious reader.

"What's with the books stacked here, Karthik?" she asked.

"Well…" he hesitated, with a smile.

"It's got to do something with a girl." she guessed.

"How can you be so sure?"

"Well, nothing other than a girl can influence you to do something that you hate so much in your life. I know how much you hate books."

"Brilliant." he said.

"Tell me about it."

He narrated all that had happened without missing an inch. Despite all the years, the memories remained fresh in his mind.

"Did you try to trace her?"

"She was not interested in me."

"That's bullshit. How can you be so sure? It's not so easy to read a girl's mind. That's why it's always safe to speak up." she said.

"Well, maybe I made a mistake not speaking up. I can't change the past."

"You may not be able to change the past, but you should not underestimate the present. Don't lose hope." she said.

"Now, tell me the address of the bookstore. I'll see if I can find her."

"I don't know the exact address. I just used to follow her and walk back on the same road."

"If you have the bill, the address should be there." she said.

"The bills should be inside the books."

"Alright, then." she said as she took one book from the bookshelf.

She shuffled through the pages and found the bill within. The bill swirled down and rested on the floor. She picked it up and found the address.

"Here, it is." she said.

"Wait a minute!" he said, and stared in disbelief.

"What's that?"

"Something is written on the back of the bill." he said in a whisper.

She immediately turned the bill and looked amazed.

'I see you watching me through your window every day. I never expected you to follow me here, but you did. It felt nice to have you here.'

Karthik couldn't believe it. Her cousin was ecstatic.

"When did you buy this book?" she asked.

"This was the book I purchased on my first visit. I can't believe she knew I was watching her."

"A girl can see even in the direction she's not looking at." she said.

"I believe that now."

"Let's see all the books." she shouted in enthusiasm.

He brought all the books to the floor. She randomly picked a book and read the bill:

'I like your shy smile. You look so cute when you do that.'

She picked up another bill.

'Your presence makes me comfortable. I really want you here every day.'

She picked up more bills and read similar messages.

Karthik was in ecstasy as her cousin kept reading more messages from the bill. So was she.

"This was the last book that I purchased." he said as he passed the book to her, somehow nervous.

'I somehow feel that you are not interested in me. Please call me if you would like to have friendship with me. Otherwise, I'll remember you as a nice person whom I didn't deserve.'

There was a phone number at the end of the message.

He was in tears when she read the last message.

"What have I done?" he whimpered in pain.

His cousin walked to him and squeezed his shoulder in assurance.

"Don't worry, everything will be alright. Let's call her."

"It's been more than five years." he said, worried.

"We'll give it a try. Call her." she encouraged.

"No, you call. I don't have the courage."

"What's her name? Quick." she asked him as she dialled the number.

"Rupa."

She waited in anxiety as it started ringing.

"Hello"

She heard a male voice.

"Hi, can I talk to Rupa?"

"She's in the kitchen. Let me call her." he said.

"May I know who is talking to me?" she asked.

"I'm her husband." he said, and kept the receiver beside the phone, calling out her name.

She immediately disconnected the call. Karthik was troubled by her worried expression.

"What happened?"

"You're too late, Karthik."

Love, unrequited

The rain played music on the thatched roof of the tuition centre, which was just a roof supported by a couple of dozen bamboo poles and crisscrossed wooden grills that formed the modest walls of the tuition centre, offering an unrestricted view of the rain. The chill drops of the rain hit the wooden grills, sprinkling fine droplets that floated in the winter breeze and caressed our faces. There were a couple of ceiling fans at such a height that they served no purpose other than producing more noise than air. Since the open walls served no purpose, the rain cramped us inside, moving us closer to each other towards the centre of the hall. Two things I liked about the rain – it fills me with mystic joy that ripples throughout my body, and the other is, it simply brings me closer to my love.

Girls and boys were seated on each side, separated by a huge gap. Since the rains invaded the space around, the seating was readjusted, bringing the boys and the girls closer. There were smiles all over. All the boys and girls thanked the rain for the opportunity. The tuition teacher hated this, but she had no other option as the rain spilled inside through the grills. I deliberately moved towards my sweetheart as close as possible. Taking the cue, he moved closer, so much that his shoulder touched mine, generating heat within my body. The chillness outside and the heat within is such an amazing feeling.

Mathematics was the most boring subject for me, and my teacher was filling the board with all crazy numbers. I pretended to take down the notes and glanced at him through the corner of my eyes. He was doing just the same, which made me blush. Rain started giving him a lot of naughty ideas. He used to drop his pen down and, on the pretext of picking it up, he used to pinch me on the calf. He brushed his arm with mine very often, and since the hall was crowded due to the rain, he occasionally wrapped his arm around my waist. When he did that, I felt ripples within, and my body shivered, sending goosebumps. For the first time in my life, I wanted the class not to end. I bowed down my head with my eyes closed and scribbled some insane numbers, pretending to work out the sums. I visualised him gently rubbing my arms and doing some naughty things. The visuals you see with your eyes closed are more beautiful and influencing than the ones you see with open eyes. The romantic atmosphere played a harp in my heart. My hand was scribbling some senseless numbers on my notebook when a friend of mine shook me.

"Class is over. Let's move."

I stared into her eyes as I was jerked out of a trance. I saw the whole world move in slow motion. Her muted lips were trying to convey something, but I was too dazed to grasp her words. I looked around at the bizarre surroundings. Everything around me dissolved into thin air like sawdust in a strong wind, and emptiness replaced my surroundings. People around me gradually turned into a puff of smoke and disappeared in the winter breeze. I turned to his side in horror to find him gradually disintegrating into the air. The romantic atmosphere turned into a nightmare. My friend was still shaking me to pull me out of my trance.

"Payal, get out of your stupid dream." my friend Sushma shouted at me.

I looked into her eyes through my tears. She was annoyed with me.

"He hung up on me today." I leaned on her shoulder and cried like a child.

The love between Tushar and me endured for 9 years. It is said that love does not fade with time, but grows stronger. But that was not the case with us. Love stayed in my mind as a taunting memory, as the reality of love for me is quite contrary to the common belief. Quarrels and disagreements had become the order of the day for us. Lives had changed, love had changed.

I still remembered the innocent Tushar when he stood hesitantly with a greeting card and a rose. He was scared to express his love. He gradually walked towards me and very unromantically handed me the card and rose. As I opened the card, he stared at me like a timid kitten. He was such an adorable and handsome boy. He was not ornate in his proposal, but I found that cute. He stole some lines from somewhere:

Roses are red

Violets are blue

You might not know

But I love you

The lines were as old as love, but I saw his pristine love in it. When I gave him a nod of approval, he returned a broad smile with wide eyes and a cute dimple. He was naïve and innocent, but he is no longer the same person. A lot has changed since then. I wish I could stop loving him, but that's an impossibility. Someone said that problems are temporary, and that had become my favourite line nowadays. My friend always advised me to give it up and move on. But how can you give up on love? Love is a promise of a lifetime, isn't it?

I didn't stop calling him. I knew he might be in some pressure as he got recruited by a top IT company a couple of years ago. I knew how demanding his job was. I expected him to spend a lot of time with me when he would be chased by his managers for some stupid deliverables and deadlines. I tried to focus on my MBA final semester, but he kept bouncing back into my thoughts.

I kept thinking why he does not love me like he did before. As I pondered over my thoughts, I looked at myself in the mirror. I was an ordinary-looking girl with a boring dress sense and old-fashioned spectacles. That's what my friends told me about my dressing style. I usually wore salwar kameez with a dupatta, which was a little outdated even for my modest town. I knew Tushar must be mingling with better-dressed people.

"But, how can a dress let you change your mind?" I argued within myself.

My friends suggested to me to improve my outlook many times. I didn't have qualms about trying different dresses. But what concerns me is that I do not want to change myself to make someone love me. I wear what makes me comfortable, even if it doesn't impress others. If something looks stylish but doesn't offer comfort to me, I would rather give it a miss. An outfit is something that you throw away at the end of the day. You carry your heart till you die. How can someone give preference to a dress over a loving heart? A few of my friends even argued that he might have fallen in love with a better-looking girl.

"You are beautiful, baby, but you don't look it. You just need a little work on yourself to make you look like an angel. Don't blame him for not caring about you when you don't care about yourself. Get rid of your granny spectacles and get some laser treatment. Quit the braid and get your hair curled. You look good with curled hair. And for God's sake, get your eyebrows waxed." Sushma advised me.

Although I listened to everyone, I hated the idea; more so because it was turning out to be a compulsion to be loved. Nevertheless, I didn't give up on my love. I believed that love always triumphs. The truth was that he's not always rude to me, but he hated the silly talk we used to enjoy. He is always straight to the point and avoided the cute banters, which used to be his trademark.

He occasionally visited the town on some weekends or vacations, and I dedicated my whole time to him. But he would not come with me to the modest roadside snack shops. He preferred some high-class café or a posh restaurant. I missed the days we used to have a hot chai and samosa chat on the roadside shop as the rainwater dripped through the holes of the worn-out tarpaulin. The melodious situational songs from the old-fashioned transistor were a treat for us. It was no longer so. We had a short chat and shared a little laughter. He occasionally joked about his job and shared some funny incidents that happened in his office. He had not changed actually, just got a little more matured. I should understand that as age goes by, people change, and I should not mistake that and hurt myself. But I must confess that I liked the old Tushar more. But old or new, he is always the person I loved the most. I enjoyed the short stint with him every time he comes home on a vacation.

When he goes back to his work, I again start to feel forlorn.

Why is separation so painful in love? What is this unnecessary fear that dominates the mind? Is it Jealousy? Is it suspicion? Or is it a premonition?

It became a routine for us – whenever he came home on a vacation, we meet up in some café. And when he went back, we kept in touch through the phone. As days passed, the frequency of his visits reduced. I understood that travelling back and forth was a tiresome affair. Even the calls reduced. I understood that he was busy with work.

My friend told me – *love is a paradox. If you hold it in your fist, it will leave you. If you let it free, it stays with you.*

I had been doing exactly the same. I was trying to hold it in my fist. I should rather let it free. Gradually, I started to accept the fact, and it did wonders for my own life. I started to focus on my studies and career. I performed better academically and also found happiness. We no longer had quarrels and arguments. Even Tushar was surprised at my sudden transformation. So were my friends. But deep down inside me, I hated the change. To accept something, you need to get used to it. I'm getting used to it. I started to participate in more extracurricular activities.

Our college girls planned a trip to Lonavala. I didn't want to go on the trip as I expected Tushar to pay a visit home. But my friends compelled me to go with them. Hence, I thought of confirming with Tushar. I tried to call him multiple times, but he didn't respond. As I continued calling, he started rejecting my calls. I thought he should be busy on a Friday evening with all the targets and deadlines. I finally gave up and sent him a message – Planning a trip with my college friends. Let me know if you are coming home this weekend.

No response yet. I was in a dilemma whether to go on with the trip or not. My friend suggested I call his home and check if he is coming or not. It pained me a lot that I had to ask someone else to know about the love of my life, who would be the first one to know everything about me. Earlier, I would be the first one to know about his plans and whereabouts. Things have changed. I called his home number and spoke to his mother, who informed me that he would not be visiting home this weekend. I had no reason to skip the tour if he was not going to be in town.

I was picked up at 8 AM, and we were set for the trip. It was such a romantic place. The journey was strewn with waterfalls all along the way, and the green landscapes offered a pleasant sight. You could always feel sprinkles of water droplets or mild rain caressing your face. I missed Tushar badly. It was a perfect retreat for a romantic couple. I saw a lot of couples enjoying the serene beauty of nature. I gaily smiled at the young lovers holding hands and drenching in the beauty of nature. I imagined Tushar and myself in every couple, and the thought stirred my heart. One such couple who were merrily jumping into the pool caught my attention. I saw the guy who hugged the girl resembled Tushar, but the girl was not me. My heart started to beat faster. Is my mind playing tricks on me? Is this a message, or a reality? When my friend Sushma saw me stop stunned in my tracks, she pulled me to walk further. My resistance brought her attention to my line of sight.

"What's Tushar doing here?" she asked.

Her words crashed me like thunder. So, it was not a delusion. Reality crushed me to pulp.

"Is there something more than friendship between the two?" I wondered.

I had tears in my eyes. I looked at my friend in stunned dismay. She looked back at me, equally stunned.

"How dare he cheat on you?" she said and started to walk towards him.

I held her arm and pulled her back. I gave her a broken smile and said, "Let it be. Let's move."

My words surprised her more than the sight. We got out of the place immediately on my insistence. My friend was furious, and strangely, I was calm. Pain had taught me more than anything in my life. For every problem, I started to analyse the reason rather than brood over the misfortune.

I got back home after the forgettable trip and pondered over the happenings. I checked my phone and found a message from him – *Sorry, dear, I have some important office deliverables this weekend. Have a nice trip.*

For the first time in my 9 years of relationship, I ignored his message. I was not angry with him, but I was lost in the mental debate.

"Don't blame him for not caring about you when you don't care about yourself."

The words resonated in my mind. Suddenly, the words made sense to me. I took a deep breath and sent a message to Sushma.

"Meet me tomorrow at my home at nine in the morning."

As I waited for her, I contemplated my plan. When Sushma arrived, I told her about my thoughts. She instantly liked it.

"Let's do it, baby." she said enthusiastically.

The next week, I was busy with my makeover. I had my eyes tested and scheduled an appointment for laser treatment. After that, I fixed an appointment with Sushma's beautician for a complete beauty package, which included a facial, eyebrow shaping, waxing, hair treatment, pedicure, and manicure. It was a packed week for me. I did a lot of shopping and let my friend choose the dress for me.

I have got myself a set of dress for my birthday, which was the following day. I wanted to invite Tushar.

I messaged him: *"Come home tomorrow, I have a surprise for you."*

I received the response from Tushar after an hour: *Sorry, dear. I have some important work. Catch you next weekend.*

Me – *Come tomorrow. You won't regret it, I promise.*

Tushar – *What's special?*

What can be more agonising than your boyfriend not remembering your birthday?

Me – *It's a surprise.*

Tushar – *It better be important, dear. I'm going to skip some important work here.*

Me – *I promise.*

The next day is supposed to be the biggest day of my life.

Tushar – *"I'm home. I plan to return tonight. Let's get the suspense unravelled, dear."*

Me – *Meet me at the paradise retreat at 7.*

Paradise Retreat was always a place for special occasions. This was a special occasion. I got ready with bated breath. I felt a little nervous, but we are always bound to do something for the first time in life. Sushma came to help me prepare for the occasion. I chose a white low-neck halter top and a purple satin skirt ending just below my knees. I chose a 5-inch purple Gucci stiletto embellished with crystals and a white cuff bracelet matching my top. A white pearl necklace adorned my neck, and the backless halter top is partially covered by the rippling curls of my hair that ended six inches below my neck. I wore glossy red lipstick.

I reserved a romantic dinner with candlelight and sent the reservation details to Tushar. He was precisely on time for the rendezvous. Though I was on time, I let him wait for some time upon the advice of Sushma. I saw him get restless as he kept waiting. I saw him pick up his phone and dial a number. My number started to ring immediately.

"Where are you? I've been waiting for so long." he said in frustration.

"Just turn around." I said as I graciously walked towards him.

He gradually turned towards my direction without much interest. When he caught sight of me, his eyes brightened in delight. His expression was a mixture of surprise and joy.

"I'm sorry, I made you wait." I apologised with a smile.

"No problem at all." he said with a broad smile.

"Is this really you?"

"I mean, you look really gorgeous. Where did you hide this beauty all these days?"

"Do I really look that beautiful?"

"You look angelic, sweetheart. Your change is terrific."

"Do you really like my change?"

"Of course, baby. I love it. I feel like getting down on my knees and proposing my love for you in this open lawn."

"You love my change! So, you didn't love me before this change?" I asked with a sarcastic smile.

His smile gradually faded, and his face turned serious.

"I had been yearning for your attention for years. And what caught your attention, was a change in my physical appearance. You can only like, but not love someone's appearance because appearance is only temporary. Love can't be based on anything temporary.

Love is not like your smartphone. You get a better phone when you get to a better position in life. Love is a mutual promise of a lifetime. You can't be loved if you don't have a deserving heart."

I unloaded all my pain in the form of words, and now I felt a huge burden lift off my heart.

"Can't you give me a second chance?" he pleaded.

"You can love a person who does not reciprocate your love, but not the one who disrespects your love. You only love my physical appearance."

"Give me a chance. Just one more."

"Once is getting fooled; twice is being a fool. I do not want to make the same mistake again." I said.

I turned around and walked back with a newfound confidence and peace of mind.

Beyond Eternity

I laid down meekly on the recliner, staring at the grand Italian Swarovski ruby red crystal chandelier as a beam of the twilight sun penetrated the bay window and pierced the blood-red crystal beads, painting the wall with eerie red patterns. The chill December breeze blew like a feeble whistle, and the chandelier beads gently danced to the wind, forming random distinct images on the wall. I tried to read the images as if they were trying to convey something to me. The images roughly looked as if Vincent Van Gogh's masterpiece 'The Starry Night' was painted in red, or at least it looked so to me. Incidentally, I have a replica hanging in my bedroom, gifted by my ex-girlfriend on our first love anniversary. The climate was cool and pleasant, but the atmosphere looked mysterious to me. Something was beyond my understanding. An inexplicable feeling stirred my heart. As the sun gradually descended over the horizon, the rays diluted, and the images on the wall slowly faded away as darkness started to engulf the sky. I still kept staring at the empty wall in deep thought. I was not able to judge my state of mind. Just when I was lost in thought, the screeching of the tyres from the driveway attracted my attention. I knew it was a date for celebration, yet I wasn't sure if it really was. I quickly walked downstairs to receive my friends who had accepted my invitation, even though they didn't know the occasion for the party, except Vasanth.

As I descended the stairs, there was a huge roar at the entrance as my friends rushed in with whistles and howling. Their excitement was expected as I rarely mingled with friends for two years. Everyone looked happy, except Prem. And I knew why. I felt it was better to let him be. Prem casually walked up to me and gently knocked me on my chest.

'Hey, mate. How are you?'

It sounded like 'buzz *off, bastard*' for me. I don't blame him entirely because I'm partly responsible for his behaviour. I stole the love of his life and then abruptly broke up with her. The reminiscence of the bittersweet past stirred my heart. But the end was what haunted me. As he walked past me, I saw something strange in his eyes. I was not able to decipher his thoughts. Vasanth, who followed Prem, patted me on my cheek and signalled me to cheer up. I just shrugged and smiled at him. He was never mean to me after all. Deva, Arjun, and Rajesh screamed as they stormed through the door.

'Here we are… Pop the bottle.' Deva shouted.

'Take a breath, skunk. You think about nothing but drinking.' Rajesh mocked Deva.

'He drinks more than he breathes.' Arjun added his part of satire.

They are always the life of a party.

'Well, well. Look who's here. I'm glad you guys made it.'

I welcomed them with a hug.

It was an occasion to celebrate. There were drinks on the table. There were friends around me, chattering and making merry. Yet, I felt like I was sitting alone. They were sitting beside me, yet I heard them from afar. It was supposed to be a party to share happiness, yet I find something jittery.

'… you lost?' Rajesh shook me out of my reverie.

My mind was full of questions, but my problem was not the answers; I was unable to comprehend the questions. I kept staring at the fizzy cubes of ice floating in the glass of Scotch, emanating countless bubbles that burst just as they approached the surface of the drink. Deva picked up the glass and emptied it in one gulp. Just as he put the glass down, he started to fill another round.

'Will you hold on for a moment and know the occasion, booze head.'

'Well, Vasanth… My ears are open.'

'You are incorrigible.' Vasanth threw the cigarette lighter at him, which missed him.

Now they are getting into endless banter. It's time for me to announce.

'Alright, guys. I'm getting engaged. I wanted to share the news to you personally.'

Even before I completed my announcement, there was a loud cheer and applause. As I completed the sentence, in the midst of cheers, the lights flickered. And in one abrupt moment, there was darkness everywhere. There was silence again; as if no one existed. It was a few seconds of silence, but it felt like eternity. An unknown fear crept through my heart. I rubbed my eyes to get them adjusted to the darkness.

'Rajesh, get the candles.' Deva commanded.

'Why always me? Haven't you got hands?'

'They are busy.' he said taking a sip from his glass.

'Then don't suggest my name. Just mind your business.'

'You are sitting on the far end.' Deva convinced Rajesh.

'Don't act smart.' he said.

'Just because I'm talking to a stupid, I can't act stupid.'

'Why did you call this drunkard to the party?' Rajesh shouted irritably.

'Come on buddy, Leave him. Go, get the candle.' Arjun requested Rajesh.

'Morons… I'm always the scapegoat.'

Rajesh got up from his seat and stopped in his tracks.

'Did you see that?' Rajesh whispered.

'What?'

'Did you guys just see that?' His whisper was louder.

'What are you talking about?'

'I saw someone move across the window.' He was almost shivering now.

'Now, now. Stop making up stories to escape your task.' Arjun said.

'I'm not lying.'

'Oh, yeah, I believe you, Rajesh. I forgot; you are someone who shits in your pants at the sight of your own shadow, aren't you?'

"It's not funny, Arjun."

'Now, you stop fighting with Arjun and get the candle.'

'I know your noble cause, Dev. You may shut up if you're not going to help. Can anyone switch on the phone torch?'

'Don't you know the rule? No phones at the party.'

'Yes, yes. That's the rule. Why don't you use the cigarette lighter?'

'It fell down somewhere. You are welcome to find it.'

'I'm not talking to you anymore, Dev.'

'Stop fighting, guys.' I intervened.

Everyone was laughing, while Rajesh still stared in the direction of the window adjacent to the stairs.

It's true that there was strong wind outside. There was every chance that he could have seen the shadow of a branch swaying outside the window, but my heart didn't take his words for a lie. He was really scared like shit.

'I'll go get it.' I rose from the couch and walked towards the kitchen, while giving one glance towards the window. As I walked away, the banter still continued.

Deva had somehow found the lighter. As I returned with the candle, I saw Dev pouring a drink, with the help of the lighter.

'You never worry about what happens around you, do you?' Arjun commented.

'Does my worrying solve any problem? No, right? Then, why should I worry when it's not going to help in any way? Remember one thing, my friend. Worry is never a solution to a problem. It's only a bonus to your already messed-up life.'

This is his first level of intoxication – Wisdom Level.

I couldn't help but smile at the transformations he attains with each level of intoxication. As I placed the candle on the table, Dev handed me the lighter. Just as I lit the candle, the room became brightly illuminated with the lights. The power was restored.

'What a timing!'

'It's symbolic, isn't it? May the darkness in your life be defeated by light, and may your life be filled with joy,' Dev blessed me, but it only evoked laughter among the guys.

Controlling my laughter, I blew out the candle. Then, suddenly, I started to feel uneasy. Something was weird. Something seemed out of place. Just as I was lost in my mental mess, I heard movement behind me. As I turned around, I saw Prem walking to the lobby from the direction of my bedroom. Nobody noticed his absence during the power cut.

'Prem is loitering in the darkness. Wonder what business he had in the dark?' Arjun spoke my heart out.

'He would have gone to use the bathroom, buddy,' Vasanth guessed.

'Could be,' Arjun replied with a hint of suspicion.

'Where are you getting lost, mate? Be with us.' Arjun shook me out of my reverie.

'Nothing,' I smiled back.

Meanwhile, Prem walked back to his seat with seriousness written all over his face and sat in his place. Rajesh timidly stared at him as if he was longing to ask him something, but he shifted his gaze hastily as Prem gave him a hard stare. Something about Prem seemed to spook Rajesh. Vasanth seemed to ignore the situation, but I felt he was pretending. A gush of wind breezed in and whistled in my ear. I have a feeling like the atmosphere is carrying a message for me.

You are being paranoid.' my inner voice echoed.

'Am I really?'

I was literally lost in my mental debate, and I was drawn out of my mental maze by the strike of the clock. I jolted back to reality and looked around to find the group making merry at the expense of Dev. It looked like he had put up a stupendous show with his drunken wisdom. The funny part was that his disclosure was for me. I was intermittently captured by some unknown fear, so I lost most of it.

Deva gulped his last peg, set his hair, tucked his shirt neatly, and wiped his face clean.

'Alright, boys, time I leave.'

'Come on, dude, what's the hurry?'

'Don't try to stop him Arjun, or you shall be the reason for his death in the hands of his wife.' Vasanth joked.

'You'll know when you get there.' Dev replied and quickly left the place while the gang still continued to laugh.

'It's purely an arranged marriage. I have never known the girl before. She's a distant relative of Vasanth.' I explained the boys about my fiancée.

'I advise you to have an open-heart discussion with her.'

'You're right, Arjun. Exactly what I did. I have given her every detail of my past, including my painful past with Anjali…'

'Just shut your bloody mouth!' Prem shouted even before I completed the sentence.

Strong wind violently gushed through the windows. The wind seemed to have picked up the fury from Prem.

'Don't you dare talk about Anjali. Don't you bloody dare, I say.'

'What wrong have I spoken about her?'

'Don't you feel guilty for what you have done? Aren't you ashamed of yourself, talking about someone who's not with us?'

'What the hell are you talking about? I haven't said anything wrong. I would say the same even if she's here.'

'You'll never get that chance…'

'Will you shut up, Prem…!' Arjun stopped him abruptly.

Prem sprang up from the couch and rushed out. Rajesh immediately followed him in an attempt to pacify him. I too stood up and tried to catch up with him, but Vasanth held me by my wrist and prompted me to sit back.

'Look, he's blabbering nonsense.'

'You know that he's blabbering, don't you? Take your seat and calm down, Sanju.'

I stared at Prem as Rajesh followed him, in an attempt to pacify him.

'Chill, buddy. I don't know what mistake he had committed. Even if he did a terrible sin, he's our friend, dude.'

'This lifetime is not sufficient for him to atone for his sins.' Prem fired back at Rajesh.

I know I had been unfair to some extent, but the break-up was mutual, and she's happily married. I didn't understand the exaggerated emotions of Prem. Even Rajesh was unable to apprehend his hyperbolic expressions.

'Let's forgive and forget. It's his happy moment.'

'Happy moment? Yes, it is, of course, a happy moment. It doesn't matter if anybody's life is destroyed.'

Rajesh stared at him in shock, as Prem continued his outrage.

'Listen, Rajesh. Blind with happiness, he's flying too high in the sky. He should realise that, no matter how high he flies, he would finally be laid beneath the ground one day.'

Prem's words sounded ominous to Rajesh. He stood there, jaw-dropped, as he saw Prem exit in absolute disdain. It was a party and it was expected to be filled with fun and laughter, but it turned into an ugly melee.

I was in total embarrassment. I was too stunned to speak.

'Take it easy, buddy. Forget everything and be happy. Don't spoil your mood with unnecessary thoughts.' Arjun took his last sip from the beer can and announced the end of the party.

'Ok, guys. Party's over. Time to leave.'

He walked up to me and gave me a reassuring hug.

'Good night, Sanju. Sleep peacefully. No worries.'

'Good night, Arjun.' I, too, bid him farewell.

Habitually, Rajesh started to clean the after-party mess.

'Leave it, dude. I'll take care of it.' I said as he started picking up the empty beer cans.

Rajesh put the empty beer cans on the table hesitantly. He walked to me and gave me a quick hug.

'Good night, pal.' Saying this, Rajesh walked away, but gradually slowed down as if he had made up his mind to speak up about something he had wanted to for quite some time. Hesitantly, he walked back to me.

'I don't know if it makes sense, but I feel something is terribly wrong.'

He's still not able to bring up what he wanted to talk about. He gave a short pause.

'I may sound bizarre. Just be careful with Prem.'

'Don't worry about Prem. His anger is not on Sanju.' Vasanth said.

'I don't think so…'

Rajesh tried to object, but Vasanth stopped him with a glare.

'You've got to get going, Rajesh. It's already late.'

He understood Vasanth's hint and left the spot immediately. Vasanth dragged the last puff and snubbed the cigarette butt in the ashtray. He lazily stood up. Meanwhile, I picked up my phone from the rack and found Prem's number.

'What are you trying to do?' Vasanth asked.

'I need to know what his problem is with me.'

'There is nothing to know. Don't imagine things.' he said, walking towards me.

I was not in a mood to listen. I just dialled his number. Vasanth snatched my phone from me and switched off the phone.

'Don't you understand what I'm saying? Listen to me, damn it. Don't talk to anyone and stop thinking about this. Forget everything and sleep well. Everything is fine.'

I heard his words, but I was partially captured by my own questions.

'Do you hear me?' He gently slapped me on my cheeks to get my attention.

I just nodded in agreement. I knew he was right.

'Good boy, Sanju.' he said, picking up his jacket from the chair and started to leave.

'Sleep well.' he shouted, walking through the exit.

It was a merry gang some time ago, which turned into a feudal mess in a while, and now it's graveyard silence. I stood in the hall all alone. But somehow, I have a feeling that I'm not alone.

I picked the empty beer cans and threw them in the trash can, gathered the soiled plates and used glasses, and dropped them in the kitchen sink. I didn't have the mood to clean them. I walked to my bedroom. Throwing my dead phone on the bed, I walked to the washroom. Though violent, the wind was silent, just with occasional whistles and howls. I relieved myself into the closet and flushed the toilet. I slowly walked to the wash basin and sprinkled cold water against my face, which pierced my skin like ice needles. The water flowing from the tap sounded like a moderate waterfall. I closed the tap and walked into the bedroom. As soon as I closed the tap, it was absolute silence which created an eerie atmosphere. As I calmly walked towards the table mirror, a strong gush of air suddenly banged the window door open. I remember securely latching the window doors and I wondered how it got opened. I sceptically walked to the window and closed it, which shut the noise away, and absolute silence prevailed again. As I stood still, getting accustomed to the deathly silence, I heard a sharp sound tear the silence of the night. When I turned around, I realised that it was the WhatsApp message notification from my mobile. I slowly walked to my bed to reach for my phone. When I walked, I felt like the sound of my footsteps didn't belong to me. They sounded alien to me. Something was strange. I picked up the phone and noticed the WhatsApp message popup. I stood transfixed for a few seconds trying to make sure that I wasn't hallucinating. I had a second look at the popup notification.

Anjali – Hi

I didn't feel excited, but I opened the message with a bit of hesitation and typed a response.

Me – Hi Anju

I called her Anju when we were in love with each other. After the break-up, I had never had any message from her, nor did I message her. I felt it strange that she messaged me after all the years, at a the most inappropriate time.

I hit backspace and retyped.

Me – Hi Anjali

Anjali – Hey, Sanju

How are you?

She replied instantly. I felt somewhat uneasy to start any conversation. I wanted to wrap up the chat as soon as possible.

Me – Good.

You?

Anjali – I'm good, baby.

Me – Nice to hear

Anjali – Hmm.

What else can I say?

Me – What do you mean?

She was skillfully drawing me into conversation.

Anjali – I hate to break it to you, dear.

But my life is miserable without you.

It's turning out to be a difficult conversation for me.

Me – I can understand Anjali.

But you have to remember that you're married.

Anjali – The fact that I'm married makes no difference at all.

I have one question for you.

Did you stop loving me when I got married?

Now, this chat was pushing me to an embarrassing situation.

Me – What?

Anjali – I never did.

Me – You shouldn't be talking like this.

You'll be in trouble if your husband knows this.

Anjali – You?

WE will be in trouble.

We already are; -)

Me – What nonsense

Anjali – He somehow got access to my secret folder.

Had a good look at our intimate pics stored there.

Me – What!!! Are you stupid, or what?

Why the heck would you store those pics?

Anjali – Well, I did

And…

Me – And what?

Anjali – He confronted me last week.

And I agreed, I'm still in love with you.

Me – Have you gone mad?

Anjali – We had a big fight.

Me – Oh my God!

Anjali – He said he'd kill us both.

He sounded serious

Me – Is this some kind of a sick joke?

Anjali – You know what?

The fight got serious.

And…

Me – And?

Anjali – He pushed me off the stairs last week.

Me – What?

My head started to spin. I was genuinely worried for her.

Me – Are you hurt?

Anjali – Just got a bump on my forehead.

Nothing else

Me – You sure you're fine?

Anjali – I'm fine, baby.

Sanjay – Ok

Be careful with him

Anjali – You be careful of him, dear. He's after you now 😊

I started to lose my cool. I'm still confused, but Anjali's words sounded credible.

I closed WhatsApp and opened the dial pad. My first instinct was to call Vasanth, but I knew he wouldn't be happy with my inquisition. I picked Rajesh's number instead.

Rajesh – Hey, dude. What's up, man?

Me – I need to know something.

Rajesh – About what?

Me – Anjali

I sensed hesitation in his voice.

Me – What's happening?

Rajesh – Look, Sanjay… It's been two years since you broke up with Anjali. You both have moved on. I advise you not to think too much about her and go to bed.

Me – Just cut the bullshit and tell me what happened?

There was silence at the other end for a few seconds. Rajesh took a deep breath and continued.

Rajesh – You know… About a week ago, Anjali fell off the stairs in her apartment and…

Me – Listen. I know that story. Just tell me about her husband, damn it.

Impatiently, I interrupted him, so much so that I almost screamed at him.

Rajesh – How do you know it!?

Rajesh was evidently surprised.

Me – Stop the nonsense and just answer my question.

He exhaled and replied.

Rajesh – I don't know much about him, but he thinks that you are the reason for all the mess. You better be careful about him. And hey, listen… Also be careful with Prem.

I disconnected the call just as he completed the sentence and threw the phone on the bed. There was some rustling of foliage outside the window, and a shadow quickly disappeared off the window pane, just a fraction of a second.

Was it my imagination?

WhatsApp notification alert drew my attention, towards my phone.

Anjali – Where have you been, my love?

Me – Relax Anjali.

Listen to me seriously.

Have you given a police complaint?

Anjali – I don't need police protection, dear.

Me – I knew you'd say that.

Come on

He already tried to hurt you once.

Anjali – Trust me, baby. It can happen only once.

Me – What do you mean by "only once?"

Anjali – Calm down, baby. Everything is fine.

Me – But let me tell you.

If he tries to hurt me, I'll hurt him back.

Don't mind

Anjali – Do you think I'll allow him to hurt you?

I'll kill him, even if he thinks of hurting you.

I hate the emotional conversation. I hated the way the conversation was heading, but I couldn't help feeling anxious about her safety.

Me – You just take care of yourself.

Anjali – You don't trust me.

Do you?

L

Me – I didn't mean that.

Anjali went offline.

Me – You there?

She's still offline. She's never changed; always hypersensitive and overemotional. I wondered why I was worried about her. I was the one who desperately wanted to end the conversation with her, but here I am worried that she went offline. I kept watching the WhatsApp screen with the hope of finding her online. For some inexplicable reason, I felt nervous. I walked to the fridge and got a tin beer and opened it. As I took a sip,

I checked the screen once again, but no messages from her. I took another sip of beer and lit a cigarette as I put the beer can on the bedside table. Once again, I picked up the phone and checked for any message notification, but I was disappointed to find none. I opened the dial pad again and contemplated whom to call.

I didn't want to call Rajesh again. He was already worried about me.

I then picked Arjun's number, who incidentally happened to be residing in the same apartment building where Anjali lived. I dialled his number, but he rejected my call. I called again, but he rejected my call again. I wondered what he was so busy with, that he kept rejecting my calls. I would have normally waited until he called back, but this was not just any other day. I kept calling him until he received the call.

Arjun – What the heck is wrong with you? I continuously reject your calls. Why don't you understand I'm not in a position to pick up the call?

Me – What are you so busy with?

Arjun – One moment.

He paused for a few seconds and then whispered in a panicked tone.

Arjun – Police

Me – Police?

Me – Tell me what happened?

He was silent again. His silence scared me.

Arjun – Murder in the apartment.

His whisper pierced through my ears and created panic in my heart.

Me – Wh… What murder? I don't understand what you are blabbering.

Arjun – Anjali's husband, was murdered in their apartment some time ago.

I felt hazy hearing his words. I felt like I had a clue about what could have happened. But when I gave it a thought, I felt lost.

Me – Damn Anjali.

Arjun – What did you say?

Me – Nothing. I'll talk to you later.

I disconnected the call without listening further. I held the phone with both my hands, unsure what to do. I opened WhatsApp and found her online.

Me – Where the hell have you been?

Anjali – Worried about me, baby?

Cho chweet

Me – Where are you now?

Anjali – In my apartment.

How can she be in an apartment where a murder has taken place and be so cool? I wondered. I'm in a dilemma now.

Anjali – What's up, baby? You look so worked up.

Me – How do you know how I look?

Anjali – Chill, baby.

Just kidding

BTW, you haven't answered my question yet.

Me – What question?

Anjali – Do you still love me?

Me – You're married, aren't you?

Anjali – That's my problem.

Me – Alright

I'm committed to a girl.

Anjali – Well…

That's again my problem, isn't it? 😈

Be right back

She's offline again. I somehow felt relaxed when I found her offline. Absolute silence shrouded the night. I walked out of my bedroom into the kitchen through the hall. The ticking of the clock matched my footsteps. I took the beer and took a sip from it. I picked a burger from the fridge and kept it in the oven to be heated. The continuous intake of beer filled my bladder. I turned on the oven and walked to the washroom.

Flushing the toilet, I walked to the kitchen slab where I placed my beer can. The oven timer alerted completion while I took a sip of the beer. I picked the burger and then walked back to the bed. The clock struck ten as I took a bite of it. Sudden gush of wind mingled with the silence of the night, which formed a deadly combination. Slowly and cautiously, I walked into the bedroom. My phone was lying on the bed with the screen facing down. I was tempted to check for any messages from her again. My heartbeat was accelerating like an incoming express train. With a lot of hesitation, I extended my hand towards the phone. The moment I held the phone, there was a loud scream. My heart almost stopped beating until I realised that it was my ringtone. I stared at the screen in horror. It was Vasanth. I didn't know why he would call me at this time when he himself asked me to switch off my phone and sleep without talking to anyone. Something was not adding up, and I didn't have the clarity of mind to understand that. I picked up the call, and I sensed a feeling of panic.

Vasanth – Sanju, Ni… Nisha. Nisha…

His voice was trembling. I knew something was terribly wrong. He was always a brave man, and his fear was sending shivers down my spine.

Me – What happened, Vasanth? I don't understand a damn thing.

Vasanth – She's no more, damn it. She's dead. Do you understand? Nisha is dead?

He was half-sobbing.

Me – Dead? Or killed?

There was silence from his end for a few seconds.

Vasanth – How the hell do you know?

Me – Not again, Anjali. Not again.

I muttered in frustration and suppressed anger.

Vasanth – What did you say?

I hesitated for a while, not sure if I should speak about all the bizarre things on my mind.

Me – Listen, I'll tell you something.

I was not sure how to use the words to explain what's on my mind.

Vasanth – Tell, tell me. I'm listening.

He waited for me to continue.

Me – Do you know that Anjali's husband has also been killed just a while ago?

Vasanth – Yes. That's bloody bizarre. So…?

Me – I have a gut feeling that Anjali has something to do with the murders.

He was shocked when he heard what I said.

Vasanth – For heaven's sake, don't say this to anyone else. You might end up in a mental asylum.

Me – In the last one hour, two murders were committed in a radius of two miles. One of the victims is Anjali's husband, and the other is my fiancée, Nisha.

Vasanth – What does it prove?

Me – Don't you understand? The connection between the two murders is me and Anjali.

Vasanth – Don't give any task to my brain. I'm already in enough confusion. Straight to the point, please.

Me – Anjali still loves me.

Vasanth – Look, Sanju. I can understand your pain. I know what you are going through. But keep calm and don't think too much about anything.

Me – Do you think I have gone bloody lunatic? I have been chatting with her for the past one hour.

He listened to me jaw-dropped and responded in a slow whisper.

Vasanth – Sanju

I sensed that he was struggling to speak something.

Me – What?

Vasanth – Do you know what happened one week ago?

Me – What?

Vasanth – Do you know she fell off the stairs in her apartment?

Me – I know… So what?

A moment of silence.

Vasanth – So what? She died, Sanju, on the spot. Anjali had committed suicide. She's no more. She's no more.

My hand couldn't hold the phone anymore. My hands shivered, and my body trembled. I didn't know if the room was spinning or if it was my head. Multiple thoughts crowded my mind.

What's happening around me?

Was Prem's wrath unreasonable?

'I haven't spoken anything wrong. I would speak the same even if she's here.'

'You'll never get that chance. It's too late…'

Murder in the apartment.

She's no more, damn it. She's dead. Do you understand? Nisha is dead?

Anjali had committed suicide.

The thoughts pounded my brain like a hammer.

Is Anjali dead? She said that her husband pushed her off the stairs. Vasanth said that she committed suicide.

Trust me, baby. It can happen only once.

Was it a murder? Was it a suicide?

If she's dead, who was chatting with me all this long? Who? Who?

Questions resonated through my hollow mind. I grabbed my ears to shut out the voice, but how could I do it when the voice was from within? Excruciating pain struck my head. I sat on the bed, holding my temple.

'Don't talk to anyone and stop thinking about this. Forget everything and sleep well.'

I remembered Vasanth switching off my phone, and I don't remember switching on my phone. I tried to stop thinking as I feared connecting the dots. As I wiggled my head to shake off the thoughts, a sharp stinging noise penetrated my ears, and my heart skipped a beat. Although this was a very familiar sound that I heard hundreds of times every day, this day was different. The sound was my WhatsApp notification. I stared at my phone, which blinked with the indication of an incoming message. My hands trembled as I picked up the phone. I dropped the phone on the bed as soon as I opened the WhatsApp message. They were just two words, which would have been very normal in ordinary circumstances. But the two words almost popped my heart out through my throat. The two words flashed in my mind repeatedly, sending shivers down my spine. The two words…

'I'm Back'

Girl on the Train

The noisy train stormed into the station with a long honk. Vendors and hawkers added to the already noisy atmosphere. Passengers stacked themselves into the train through the narrow entrances. Luckily, I didn't have to compete with the fierce mob. I took my time and calmly walked towards the compartment which had a seat reserved for me. I knew that the reserved compartments were also not completely spared, but I can at least be sure that I have my seat for myself. The first thing I did after reaching my coach was to check the reservation chart. Since I already knew my seat number, you should know what a single male in his early twenties would be checking for. Like always, it was not something that pleased me. I pushed through the standing crowd and located my seat number, expecting to find an old lady occupying the seat beside me. I was not wrong. I know very well about my rotten luck. She greeted me with a smile, sitting at the window seat which was actually mine. I allowed her the window seat with a smile and took the middle seat which was apparently hers. I was accustomed to this chivalry in my years of experience in train journeys, although I hated giving up my window seat. The passenger details of the third seat were not mentioned in the reservation chart, which may be due to cancellation of reservation at the last moment. I picked up my mobile headset and got prepared for yet another dreary journey.

Just when I was about to plug my ears with my headset for music, I saw a beautiful girl sail through the crowd. Music started playing even before I put my headset on. Every step she walked closer to my seat widened my smile. She got seated a few rows before mine, and a middle-aged man in a dhoti and khaddar shirt occupied the seat beside me. I reminded myself about my rotten luck. I shrugged with a smile and put my headset on with my eyes closed. Music kept me occupied for some time. The hustling of the crowd at the next station drew my attention. The seat beside me was vacant. I assumed that the man got off at that station. I saw the TTE at the end of the compartment. I wanted to let the ticket examination be done before I get back to my music as I didn't want to be disturbed again in between. I saw the ticket examiner dutifully check the tickets of everyone in order. As he proceeded, I saw that a few people vacated their seats and stood near the doorway, and a few people with unreserved tickets occupied the seat by paying the reservation charge. He then went to the girl who swayed my mind a little while ago. She didn't seem to have a reservation, as she too vacated the seat, which got occupied by another lady who seemed to have reserved that seat. I didn't know why I was so keen on her. The TTE wrote a slip for her, and she paid the reservation charge. I saw the girl remove the bags from her place and walk in my direction, checking the seat numbers. To my delight, I saw her place the bags on the rack above my row and take the empty seat beside me. I switched off the music and kept the headset in my bag. I had a feeling that I wouldn't need them anymore. I showed my ticket to the TTE, and he moved further.

She was very beautiful, and I'm not exaggerating. She must be around 5.4' tall, but a perfect body wrapped in simple blue body-fit jeans and a plain white half-sleeved cotton shirt, yet oozed elegance. Her presence delighted me, but her beauty made me nervous. She sat beside me, but she didn't seem to be a friendly person. I wanted to make a conversation with her, but she never allowed me to make one as she didn't even respond to my smile. But her silence didn't spell arrogance. I thought she didn't notice my smile. I agree I was not an expert in wooing girls, but unable to speak a word is shameful, I thought. I didn't know where to look or what to do. I was trying too hard to act natural, but failed terribly. The other lady at the window seat noticed my inconvenience.

"You don't look alright. Can I help you?" she offered help.

Her intention was genuine, but I hated her because I felt embarrassed being exposed. Thankfully, the girl didn't notice the conversation. I just smiled in response to the old lady, nodding that I'm okay. When she continued her observation outside, I felt relaxed. Suddenly, I sensed an uncomfortable commotion beside me.

"Is she experiencing the same as I did?" I wondered.

I thought this was the right chance to start a conversation.

"Are you alright? Can I help you?" I asked her.

The old lady beside me immediately looked at me and then turned back with a knowing smile. She didn't respond to my question. Instead, she quickly got up from her seat and looked around. I was scared that she was looking for the TTE to complain about me. She walked towards the exit behind me. I didn't feel like checking where she walked, but the old lady turned around, watched her for a few moments, and then turned back.

"I guess she is in some trouble, my child," she told me.

"What?" I didn't understand.

"She looks mentally disturbed. Something is tormenting her. Maybe something's not well with her family," she said.

I turned around and saw that she was washing her face at the wash basin. She was holding her forehead, covering her face for some time. Something looked wrong.

"What could be wrong?" I asked her.

"You have to find that out."

"I don't think she will answer me."

"Look, child. If you want a girl's attention, you should know what to talk and when to talk. If your approach is right, she will respond." she said.

I was so grateful to the lady. She wiped away my nervousness and doubts. I waited for her to return. When she returned, she wore a pair of dark goggles. One look at her told me that the lady was right. I thought I should talk to her.

"Is there…"

Just when I was about to talk to her, her phone rang. She took the phone and again walked to the washroom area and kept talking. After she disconnected the call, she called another number. She didn't stop making calls. My neck pained because I craned backwards to look at her. When I was about to get up to walk towards her, the old lady stopped me and asked me not to intrude into her conversations.

"I know you want to help her. Give her some time, child." she said.

I restrained back in my seat. I was really worried for her. I didn't know how long she was on calls, but she didn't give a break. After what felt like eternity, she walked back to her seat. I was hesitant to talk to her.

"You look to be very disturbed. What's the problem, child?" the old lady asked her.

She turned towards the lady and looked at her for a few seconds.

"My father is hospitalised, and he is in a serious condition. He had an accident and lost a lot of blood. The blood bank doesn't seem to have his blood group."

"What's his blood group?" I interjected, after gaining courage.

"B Negative." she said without looking at me.

"That's not my group, child. What's your group, son?" she asked me, engaging in the conversation.

"My group is A positive, aunty." I said.

"But I think that shouldn't be a problem. I have details of an NGO who can help you with it."

She suddenly turned towards me with interest.

"Can they really help?"

"I trust them because they helped my friend's uncle during an emergency. They conduct blood donation camps and also maintain a database of interested donors. Even if they don't have blood in the bank, they know where to get it."

She removed her goggles, and her eyes shone in newfound hope.

"Can you give me the details?" she asked me.

"Sure, I have the details in a WhatsApp message. I'd like to share with you." I said, picking up my phone.

As I searched the message, she gave me her phone number. I can't believe that she was giving her phone number to me. I took her number and shared all the necessary information with her. However, the information was not sent to her as there was no network.

"Did you send me?" she asked.

"Yes, I did. But no network." I said.

Just then, the train came to a halt. To my bad luck, it was her stop. She immediately pulled her bag from the overhead rack and rushed through the crowd, forgetting to thank me. Or did she think I didn't do anything that deserved thanks? Just as I saw her leaving, with disappointment, the old lady tapped on my shoulder.

"Everything will be alright," she said, and rose to leave.

I took the window seat as she walked away from her seat. It looked like everything happened in a flash. I recollected all that happened in a span of four hours or so. So much had happened in that short time. As I stared outside the window, I saw the old lady waving at me.

"Take care, son," she said.

I smiled at her and waved back. But I was not able to find the girl anywhere. Maybe she went the other way. I had travelled many hundreds of times on the train, but this experience was so special. Although what had happened was the first time for me and was also totally unexpected, I hoped for something better. But I knew that life had been fair with me. Just the heart does not have any restraints. I wish she had stayed longer. I wish we had developed a friendship. I wish we would fall in love. I could wish for anything.

I pulled the headphones from my bag again and started to play my favourite melodies. I just shut my eyes and didn't care who sat beside me thereafter. The train finally pulled to a halt. I knew that it was my stop. I didn't rush as it was the last stop. I leisurely picked up my luggage and walked out after the violent mob scrambled out of the train.

She stayed in my mind for many days. She made such an impact just at the first glance. Gradually, I forgot about the incident and got on with my life. Some people come to stay, but some people come and go, making a deep impact.

One fine day, when I was sitting in a park and listening to music, I got a message on WhatsApp. The number was not stored in my phonebook. I also didn't have a history as I regularly clean up unwanted stuff. But the message hinted that I knew the sender.

"Thank you for your timely help."

I had not helped many, which made it easier for me to find out.

"Are you the girl on the train?" I asked without any pretension.

"Yes."

"I'm glad I could help. It cost me nothing."

"It might have cost nothing to you, but it saved someone who is everything to me."

"Nice to hear that."

"I'm sorry I didn't have the thought to thank you at that time. It shouldn't have taken me this long."

"I didn't expect thanks. I was only glad I could help."

The conversation continued, and friendship grew between us. She's an intelligent and lively girl, unlike the impression she made on that day. I began to fall in love with her. I was hesitant to express my love for her. I gathered my courage and proposed my love for her one day.

"Love is such a great feeling that cannot be declared through a brief social media interaction." She replied and I was disappointed.

"But I know you are a nice guy. Let's be friends for some time. If we feel that we could live together for a longer time, then we shall make a decision," she said.

With hope in mind, I waited for good to happen.

Game of Messages

"I understand sir. If I were in your position, I would have felt the same. I understand how terrible it is when a call drops in the midst of some important conversation. Rest assured, sir, we are doing our best to improve the network. I shall take your case with very high priority and get your bill revised accordingly."

All the frustrated dialogues were to get a waiver from the bill.

"Sure, sir. You shall pay the bill only after your case is solved. It was a pleasure serving you. Thank you for calling Air Voice. You have been talking to Gagan."

The floor was buzzing with a thousand voices. The most common word that hovered around the floor was 'sorry, sir.' The constant usage of the headset sometimes made my ears numb. The Avaya headset that plugged my ears delivered the relentless abuses of an irate customer. To escape the ire of the irate customer, we, at the customer care, splurge innumerable fake promises, only next to our politicians. The problem with a new service provider in establishing a network is that they give high promises but don't deliver as promised. Actually, it's quite impossible. But the customers believe whatever these companies promise and jump into the offers. It's the customer care which is the scapegoat. I quite got used to the abuses. We were taught during our soft skills training that we should face all the calls with a smile, no matter what. We were trained to take abuses and paid to take abuses.

My Avaya says that I still have three minutes to complete my shift. I wondered if I should take another call.

"Never pick up a call during your last few minutes."

That was the common mantra. It was a long day. My shift was about to end. It was three minutes short of 4 AM. The call flow was less, but still, I didn't want to risk getting caught by any drunk asshole who called the customer care just for fun. I had exhausted my break time. Still, I didn't care. I had had enough fun for the day. So, I put myself on break mode and leaned back on my ergonomic chair. The second it struck the 4th hour, I threw my headset and logged off. Every day was an achievement.

The floor was almost deserted as the expected call rate was low. Nearly six hundred people occupied the single floor. Although we work together, we seldom knew people outside the team.

I leisurely walked along the floor towards the exit, as I needn't rush for my cab. I had ample time as I had logged off on time. I have a silly fancy of observing others' workplace. I find it amusing to guess their character by their workplace. At one desk, I see a lot of torn bits of papers. I guessed the person was torn apart by one of the customers. At one desk, I found four cups of coffee. It told me about the efforts taken to stay awake. The chair was reclined, and the trash can was inverted at one desk, which told me that the person was so thick-skinned, hence relaxed.

In the endeavour of desk observation, I came across one desk that intrigued me. The place was very neatly maintained, unlike other places. There were some indoor croton plants and a calendar with inspirational quotes for each month. There was a whiteboard which bore a message in beautiful handwriting – *Today was a beautiful day.*

Beside the whiteboard, there was a wooden whiteboard eraser on which a pair of open wings was engraved. I picked up the eraser, wiped the message on the board, and wrote the message: *Workplace speaks a lot about the worker's character. I don't need to say it's beautiful. Wish you a beautiful tomorrow.*

Unknowingly, it lightened my heart. I forgot all the frustrations that wracked my mind. I walked out of the floor, whistling my favourite song.

I wanted to share the event with my friends, but they had already left for the shift by the time I reached the apartment we shared. It had been nearly four years since I joined here as a fresher, and since then my team had been changed and shuffled multiple times. But I was lucky that two of my very close friends remained in my team or moved with me to different teams. However, since we worked in different shifts and had offs on different days, we rarely met. By the way, I wanted to share the event with my friends because I share everything with them, not because this was of great importance. I slept at 4:45 AM. The call centre life doesn't allow us to respect our circadian clock. We're neither nocturnal nor diurnal. We slept during the day when we were in night shifts and during the night when we had day shifts. We were not only selling our skill but also health in exchange for a meagre salary. However, we learnt to be happy with our lives.

The next day was no different. The same calls, same customers, and same fake promises. After the shift, I followed the same procedure on my way back to the exit, observing all the desks. Incidentally, I came across the desk where I wrote my message as I walked through the maze of cubicles.

Hope you have a beautiful day too.

That was an open conversation. I had to respond. I thought of writing in response to the message, but then it occurred to me that the next day was Friendship Day.

Perfect opportunity to send a friend request.

Friendship is a special bond that binds two strangers together forever.

'Happy Friendship Day'

The next day after work, I went straight to that cubicle, ignoring the others.

'Friendship works in mysterious ways. It is a plant that grows even in the most improbable conditions.'

Happy Friendship Day, my friend.'

True, it is. I never expected friendship with a person whom I have never seen. I don't know if the person is a boy or a girl, young or old. I knew nothing, but some friendship developed between us in improbable circumstances.

I left for the day with a pleasant feeling. It had been a routine for me every day. Our friendship grew day by day. Neither of us thought of exchanging more details about ourselves. I was in the night shift, and she was in the early morning shift. The friendly conversations continued for a few more days. After a few weeks, there was once again a team shuffle. I really didn't understand why the teams should often be re-organised. In my opinion, the rapport built over time would be destroyed in a moment. Maybe they have their own administrative reasons.

We had a new team and a new bay. We occupied our workplaces and began to work on the calls without delay. Our bay was at a different location from our previous one. It was quite close to the exit. I was happy that I need not walk that long to get out of the floor. Days were busy after the latest team shuffle. I had been enrolled for new product training, following which I was promoted to the team lead position. I considered the new workplace and the new team lucky for me. The new team was also a congenial bunch. Everybody looked excited to work with me. I was busy in my new role in a more comfortable shift. In the excitement of all the positive happenings, I forgot my mysterious friend with whom I shared an inexplicable bond of friendship. I felt ashamed of myself for ignoring a friend in the moment of glory.

I immediately walked to the cubicle, but the sight of the cubicle didn't excite me like it usually did. The whiteboard was empty. The desk, which looked so beautiful to me, no longer seemed so. Did I annoy my friend? Was I mean by disregarding my friend in my moment of joy? I had questions in my mind that gave annoying answers.

'How have you been?'

I wrote on the board as I didn't know what more to write.

Next day was a busy day for me. In fact, after taking up the lead role, I was very tightly packed with meetings, reports, emails, escalations, etc.

'You can never be busy for a friend.'

With this thought, I walked to that cubicle, but was disappointed to find the whiteboard wiped clean. I knew that I deserved it. But I never hesitated in apologising.

'I'm sorry. I was busy for the last few days.'

I wrote this message hoping it would work.

The next day, I walked straight to that cubicle before mine to read the response.

'GET LOST'

When I read the message, I was heartbroken. I thought it was very rude to respond in such a way.

'I won't trouble you anymore. Good luck.'

I replied to the message and left the place with a heavy heart. The excitement that I experienced with the new changes faded. I never turned to that cubicle thereafter. I tried to keep myself occupied with my new job, but somehow, sometimes, my guilty conscience pricked me. I forgot the episode gradually, but something told me that I had missed a good friend.

'I had previously fought with many of my friends and maintained distance for longer times, and few of them never became my friends again. I never worried about them for so long. What was so special about that friend?'

Questions started to haunt me. My team had started observing my change of behaviour. They enquired about it a few times, but I just brushed it off, saying I was just a little stressed. I regained my normalcy and started to get back on track. My team excelled in quality and productivity. I received a lot of appreciation for the excellent job that I had been doing. A couple of my team members won awards for their performance.

'May I call Ranjan upon the stage to receive the award for the best associate for overall productivity.'

'May I call Shruthi to the stage to receive the award for the best associate for overall quality.'

'May I call Gagan to the stage to receive the best team award.'

There was roaring applause. This was my first big success at the job, and I was proud of my team who made it happen. I thanked my whole team for making it happen and promised a team dinner to celebrate the success. I wanted to congratulate the winners personally. So, I thought of walking to their cubicle to congratulate them. I walked to Ranjan, who had nerdy looks with thick spectacles and a lean body frame. I patted his back and then walked up to Shruthi's cubicle. She's a beautiful girl with bright eyes and a sparkling smile. I shook her hand and wished her greater success. I appreciated her cubicle for neatness, but something struck my sight that sucked me into it. There I saw the croton plants, the same calendar, and also the same wooden eraser beside the whiteboard.

'Today is my happiest day. I miss my friend to share the joy.'

When I read the message on the board, it brought me more joy than the award that I received some time back. I just gave her a smile and then returned to my cubicle. I didn't know how to proceed. I suddenly felt nervous. I waited for her to leave, pretending to be busy. Once she left, I walked up to her cubicle and erased the whiteboard. For the first time, my hand shivered to write my mind.

'I missed my friend as much. Glad, I found her back.'

It gave her a hint that I knew her. I didn't want to prolong the hide-and-seek anymore. The next day, I reached our workspace earlier than her to watch her reaction when she read the message on the board. When I saw her walk to her desk, I stood in a position that I wouldn't miss her expressions. I waited with bated breath as she sat on her chair and settled herself before having a look at the whiteboard. When she looked at the whiteboard, her expression elated me. She placed her palms on her mouth in joy. As my sight was transfixed on her, she met my gaze which matched her state. With the unexpected surprise, she nodded her head in question. I slowly walked to her desk, and as I nodded my head in affirmation, she held my hand. I got a feeling that our hands would be held together for a really long time. And they did.

Life is the Gift

The clacking of the keyboard filled Sam's cubicle. It was half past twelve, and only one cubicle was lit on the whole floor. Sam gave a short relief to the keyboard as he stared at the code that appeared on his screen. As he scanned the code, he took a bite of the Subway burger without removing his sight from the screen. He then took a long sip of coke to wash the burger down his throat, all the while scrutinising the code. The code is not a big challenge for him, but his eyes refused to cooperate as they had been staring at the system for a straight fourteen hours. He blinked a couple of times to adjust his sight to the dim night light. As he concentrated back on the system, he noticed a message alert.

Strange; because he was supposed to be the only person in the building, barring the security people and the server maintenance team. The code demanded his attention, but his tired mind preferred a change. He opened the chat window and saw a message: *'Hi.'*

"Who is this sender?" he wondered as he saw the name 'Ritika Deshpande.'

He had been in the company for 2 years but had never heard the name.

"And what on earth is she doing at this hour of the night?"

"Should be from the maintenance team," he thought.

"Hi." he replied.

He thought again about her and wondered who she was. He knew that he had never heard the name before and wished to know about her.

"Which team do you belong to? Never heard your name before!"

"You never had time to notice people around you. All the time, you look at nowhere other than your computer." He couldn't deny that. Now, his curiosity peaked. He wanted to ask many questions, but his mind is clouded.

"I know you have a lot of questions to ask, but your brain is jammed. Why don't you jump out of your seat for a cup of coffee?"

"Sure."

The break was very much needed for his tired mind and body, but seeing her was more tempting than the coffee.

"I'll see you in the cafeteria in 5 minutes."

Her status changed to *'Be right back.'* He didn't waste time in doing the same. He checked the time and locked his system.

He was surprised when his legs led him to the washroom. He stared at his dishevelled state in the mirror.

"You can't meet a girl for the first time like this."

He washed his face and combed his hair with his fingers, and then neatly tucked in his shirt. One last look at himself in the mirror, and he was satisfied with what he saw.

"Better," he thought.

The watch suggested that six minutes have elapsed.

"Damn! Meeting a girl for the first time, and you are already late by a minute."

"Wait a minute. It's just a casual meet, not a date."

"It's definitely not a date. My mind is too tired to think sanely. I surely need the break."

He shrugged off his meaningless mental debate and walked casually to the cafeteria. He looked around and then back at his watch. It was ten minutes past the appointed time. He pulled a metal chair and sat as close to the entrance as possible. The noise caused by the pulling of the chair woke the canteen keeper.

"Can I get something for you, sir?"

"I'll call you when I need," he said curtly.

Involuntarily, he kept checking the entrance every five seconds. The canteen keeper observed his strange antics and wondered who he was waiting for. He knew very well that no one from his circle, except him, stays this late.

Coming to the conclusion that she would not come, he decided to have his cup of coffee alone.

"Get me a cup of coffee."

He got his cup of coffee and walked to the open terrace. The cool breeze washed his mind of his tiredness. The heat in his eyes cooled off, and his muscles relaxed by the short walk on the terrace. He leaned back on the parapet wall and outstretched his hands, still thinking about her. He never thought about anyone that hard. She surely had quite an impact on him. The cool breeze and the intriguing thoughts made him lose track of time. The more he thought about her, the more she played on his mind, and more questions arose. He was determined to find answers to the haunting questions. Immediately, he placed the cup at the nearest table and rushed to his computer. Without wasting a second, he unlocked the system, only to be disappointed. Her status showed offline.

"Maybe, she was annoyed because of my delay."

"It's okay if we wait for hours for a girl, but she can't wait for ten minutes."

He also logged off his system as he no longer had interest to continue with the boring codes.

All night, he kept thinking about her. How would she look? How would her voice be? Was she short or tall, fair or dark, lean or plump? He thought of calling his colleagues to know about her but again decided against it. He resolved not to reveal it until he was sure about the relationship.

The first thing he did the next morning after logging in was to check for any missed conversation. There was none. He thought of finding her on the office communicator. Just then, a message alert beeped at the right lower corner of his computer with the name he was looking for. He did not open the message immediately. He was guessing what the message would be. When he read the message, he cherished the feeling for a few seconds, his lips curved into a broad smile without his knowledge, which didn't go unnoticed by his colleagues.

"Looks like someone's happy today," one of his female colleagues commented as she passed by.

He immediately kicked his chair closer towards his monitor, blocking it from her sight. He gave a customary smile and waited for her to move away from his cubicle. Just when he made sure that he was not being pried upon, he glanced towards his monitor to read the message again.

"Sorry for last night. I had to leave early due to some urgent work."

When he read the message again, he was glad that she was not against meeting him.

"No problem," he replied.

Her status was 'away.' He wanted to wait until she came online.

"Can we meet today?" he wanted to ask just as she came online.

"Can we meet up at 1 for lunch?" she delighted him by speaking his mind.

There was no way he would deny the offer.

"Sure"

Out of curiosity, he forgot something, which he understood only when he went to the food court at the appointed time. He had never seen the person he was supposed to have lunch with. He felt like a fool as he stared at the bustling crowd. She knew him, and that was his saving grace.

"Care to join for lunch?" he heard a voice behind him.

He turned around in joy, which fizzled off in a second when he found the same girl who had commented while he was chatting with his mysterious girl.

She was a fair girl, just about five and a half feet. She stood on four-inch heels, which brought her almost close to his equal height. Her sparkling teeth were complemented by her glossy red lips. Her slender body is tastefully adorned in a simple tunic top and a pair of faded denim jeans. He didn't even know her name, although they belonged to the same project, as she didn't report to him.

"Well, I'm waiting for a friend."

"I can see that," she giggled meaningfully. He didn't like that.

After a few minutes wait, he silently walked to a table far away from his colleague. He scanned around the food court, hoping to see if someone was waiting for him. But he saw no one who looked to be waiting for someone. He was annoyed that she failed to meet him for the second time. He had a quick lunch and returned to his desk, determined to check her profile in the company portal to know how she looked. Just as he logged in, he received a message alert.

"You had your lunch as if you were starving for days!" She messaged with a naughty smiley.

He was not amused by her taunts.

"If you didn't want to have lunch with me, why did you invite me then?"

"I'm sorry, I didn't mean to annoy you. I thought of waiting for a while, hoping you would find me. But when I thought of calling you, my manager insisted on having lunch with him. By the time I got rid of him, you were gone. I even skipped my lunch halfway to catch up with you, but you were gone."

He cursed himself for making a hasty judgement about her.

"Why don't you finish your lunch now?"

"I'm not feeling hungry anymore. I'll probably leave for early snacks."

"I'll probably join you for snacks then. By the way, did I see you at the food court?"

"Well, you could have seen me," she teased him.

"Did my glance pass her? Did I miss someone who was checking me out?" He tried recalling the faces he saw in the food court, but his memory couldn't fetch a face that was curious about him.

He immediately resumed his search for her profile.

"Hey, I have a proposal."

"What is that?"

"I know that you don't know me by my face. I challenge you to find me without checking for my picture on my profile. One week's time. And I fix the meetings."

"Sounds interesting,"

"I also have a surprise gift for you. I promise you won't regret it."

He was not the one to refuse a challenge. The surprise gift she promised further intrigued him.

"Deal," he agreed.

Gentleman, he was, that he stuck to the deal.

He began to think about her conversation all night. His thoughts were particularly about the gift she mentioned. He did not realise that she had begun to occupy his mind so much. The first thing he did the next day was to have a haircut and a neat shave. He had a long shower and applied a liberal scoop of hair gel. For the first time, he chose his dress consciously from his wardrobe and then pressed his shirt and trousers. He almost emptied the deodorant spray all over himself. It was a new phase of his life. This was the first time in all the years that he spent so much time on anything apart from codes. He loved the change. His roommates stared at him with half-open eyes from their beds and wondered what had happened to him. The two roommates who shared the apartment with him smiled at each other meaningfully and wrapped the blanket back over themselves.

His colleagues were surprised by the sudden change in him.

"You look very handsome today," He was greeted for the day by one of his lady colleagues with a compliment that made him blush.

They made multiple appointments. He used all his investigative skills to find her out. Every time they fixed a meeting appointment, he would take notice of all the faces that he saw. Every next time, he would deduct the faces that were not common for both instances. But he realised that it's a long shot, as he had to deal with hundreds of faces. He failed every time. He then realised that every time, he was the one searching for her. It then occurred to him that she would also be checking out for him when he did that for her. So, he tried a ploy.

At their next appointment at the food court, he did not go to the dining place. Instead, he hid at an inconspicuous spot and watched for a hint. He scrutinised the crowd to find the girl he was appointed to meet every day but never met. He then observed a girl restlessly glancing at the entrance.

Bingo

He came out of his hiding place and victoriously walked towards her. She then glanced in his direction and waved. He raised his hand to wave back at her, but someone walked past him, waving back at her. When the man got seated opposite to her with a smiling reception from her, he knew that his plan had failed, once again. It only amused him. He laughed at his crazy ideas. He began to walk back to his workplace and took one look at the couple having coffee together, which brought a subtle smile to his lips. He liked this game. He felt lighter and happier with the new phase of his life. His mind became less burdened. He laughed and smiled more. He took care of his looks. Every day he looked forward to something exciting. His life changed. He never knew a girl could change his life so much. He liked the life he was living then. He tried a new trick every day and eventually lost. But the failure cheered him up. He never knew that failure could cheer someone.

In love, even failure is cherished. Wait a minute! Is this love? Don't know yet.

But what else can cast such a magical spell on someone?

He didn't care as he was busy experiencing the magic. He was no longer the nerd he used to be. He grew younger by day. He finally found his balance in life. His colleagues also appreciated his change, nevertheless, intrigued by the reason. He moved friendly with his team.

"Hey, Zombie. Congratulations on getting back to life." his friends mocked him.

True, it was. He felt like a zombie himself. Now, he didn't make any effort to convince himself that it was not love. The hide-and-seek would last for only one more day. The next day was the final day of the challenge. He was both restless and excited about the outcome of the challenge. That day was no different as he failed to find her. But he knew he would see her the next day. Hence, he was not bothered about the failure.

"You lost the challenge," she pinged with taunting smileys.

"Don't worry. You'll have your surprise before the end of the day," she promised.

It was time to leave, but still no sign of surprise. He thought of checking out with her, but found her offline. With a hint of disappointment, he logged off and left for the day. He yanked his shoes off and pushed open his apartment door, but it was dark.

"What the hell!" he cursed.

Just then, the light flickered and to his surprise found the apartment filled with decorations and writing on the wall:

HAPPY BIRTHDAY

In all the excitement, he forgot his birthday. His colleagues swarmed him, singing the birthday song. The rest of the night was eventful, with the gang of friends creating frenzied havoc, applying cream all over his face, and throwing glitter papers all over the place. It was a memorable night for him, only that he missed the mystery girl. He was sure that he would meet her the next day.

Next day, he started for the office early. He waited for his customary morning greeting, but to no avail. Her status still showed offline. He then remembered promising her that he would not check her profile for one week, which was the stipulated challenge period. He immediately opened his company portal and typed 'Ritika Deshpande' and hit the search button. He eagerly awaited as the processing wheel spun and spun. Meanwhile, he started imagining how she would look. It took longer than usual, hiking his excitement.

"Happy birthday, Sam," his manager, Vikas, wished him.

"You look so curious, man. What's up?"

"Do you know Ritika?"

"What?"

"Ritika Deshpande."

The manager looked a little uncomfortable with his question.

"Why do you want to know?"

"Tell me, Vikas. Do you know her?"

"She was an ex-employee. She was part of your team before you joined."

"What do you mean? Does she work here no more?"

"Actually, she is no more."

Sam stood frozen by the horrifying revelation.

"She died three years ago due to cardiac arrest. Too much work pressure." he briefly narrated the story.

"As a matter of fact, you are using the same system she used when she was here," he said and left the place as he was no longer comfortable to discuss the matter.

He stared at his system as the search ended.

'No results found.'

He had goosebumps with the revelation. His head started spinning with a recap of the incidents that seemed surreal now. Everything that had happened for the last few days was like a dream. Just then, his computer beeped with an incoming message. With shaky fingers, he opened the message.

There was a birthday greeting card with a message.

I promised a gift today. There can be no gift greater than life. While you get occupied with some important work, you forget the essence of life – Happiness. When something you do cannot fetch you happiness, all the money, pride, and glory you earn are of no use. Do your work, but spare some time to look after yourself and your beloved ones, spare some time to be happy, spare some time to live. Treasure the gift. Don't let the work kill you.

Work to live, don't live to work.

Wish you many more smiles and sparkles. Happy Birthday.

The live greeting card threw glitters and sparkles and fizzled off. He checked for the greeting card in his inbox, but it was not there. He checked for the chat log; it was missing too, but the message got etched on his mind like a writing on a rock.

Deception Point

Facebook has become an integral part of my life. For me, it's like a window through which I see the world. It has become a compulsion and addiction. Why has Facebook become so famous? Is it because of your curiosity to know others? Or is it because of your obsession to be heard, liked, and followed by people? I do not have the audacity to probe into my greatest passion. I just live through Facebook. Every day, my friends list grows bigger and bigger. I wondered many times how a little window can bring friends across the vast world together in a small circle. It has, in fact, packed the world in a box. I have found many friends whom I thought to have lost forever. But again, I get requests from people I don't know. The world is such a friendly place – I wondered. It also offers an opportunity to live the inexpressible hidden side of yours in the identity you fancy. For me, it's the start of the day and end of the day. I consider it my duty to update my day-to-day happenings without fail on my wall.

It's a beautiful day.

Feeling depressed

Feeling happy

Cooked palak paneer today. Looks yummy.

Salary day, the only exciting day at the office.

Leaving for Manali with family. Holiday time.

It was literally a live relay of my life. It was funny that I conversed more with my family through Facebook Messenger and WhatsApp Messenger, more than I did in person. You are never far away from family – I thought proudly. I never cared to think if the social networking had brought people together or become a wedge between people, as it sounded ironic. It has so much coalesced with my life that a short interruption with the network would drive me crazy. It sometimes scares me how my life would be without it. I again wondered how my parents and grandparents lived without it in their days.

I post pictures of myself and my family every now and then. I take selfies from every damn place, from a restaurant to a restroom. Every time I post a picture, I would be counting how many people liked it. The number of likes defined my worth for me. I take note of who liked my posts and who didn't. I only liked back those who liked mine. I believed that only those who liked my posts are my friends. I hated people who didn't.

I made it a rule to update every happening in my life, live. If you want to know about me, you just visit my Facebook profile. You'll know every detail of my life. I talk to friends every day, though I don't meet them regularly. I also talk to strangers who became my friends on Facebook. In addition to this, Facebook suggests friends who might be of interest. I would pry into their profiles every now and then. It's a kinky affair checking into the girls' profiles and knowing about them without their knowledge.

It was a Sunday. I had chatted with some friends until 3 AM. Since the internet connected every corner of the world so seamlessly, my body demanded to get adjusted to various time zones of the world. We have a group conversation with friends across the US, Europe, and India. I still don't remember what we chatted about, but it was very exhaustive. I don't even know when I fell asleep. It was a known fact among the friends' group that if someone drops without announcing, assume that they have fallen asleep. I ran my hand along the bed even before I opened my eyes, searching for my phone. I opened my eyes after I found the phone. I blinked a few times as I stared into the bright screen, and the first thing I did was to check the conversation track which I left last night. It went on until 5 AM. I went back to my messages and wondered how I didn't remember what I chatted about for a couple of hours before I fell asleep. I chatted in a subconscious state. I laughed as I ran through the conversation. It was such fun. I again thanked social media for enabling me to get connected with all my friends, no matter how far they are.

I began my routine of going through all my social networks to check what has happened in the last 5 hours. I had nearly 175 WhatsApp messages, not many of them useful though. As I checked my Facebook, which occupied a larger share of the online time, I saw 24 notifications, 12 messages, and one friend request. The new friend's name was Jasmine. I'm sure I don't know anyone by that name. When I opened the profile of the new friend, I was pleased to find the profile picture of a beautiful girl posing with a luminous smile. New friends always excited me, especially when they were girls. I did not waste a second in accepting the request. I checked for mutual friends and found that we had three mutual friends, but all three were strangers to me. Well, technically I can't call them strangers. They are my friends now, aren't they? The first thing I would do when I get a friend request from someone I don't know is to go to the about page. I did the same. But not many details there, not even a location. I checked the gallery for her pictures. They were a stunning set of photos. She could easily pass as a model. I checked her status and found her online. I was tempted to ping her, but I do not want to seem desperate. I finished my morning chores and then lazily plopped down on the couch, retrieving my phone to check for any notifications. It was a default physical activity that doesn't need a command from the brain. Again, I was tempted to chat with my new friend. Now I didn't care about seeming desperate. I quickly opened the chat window and found her still online. I began my social network interaction with the newfound friend.

Hi

I didn't get any reply for some time. I wondered if I had made any mistake by taking the first step.

'*Hesitating to take the first step is the biggest mistake in relationships,*' I enlightened myself.

Just when I was about to close my messenger, I got a message notification, which I opened without any delay.

Hi

Now, the greeting is done. How do I proceed further? Do I ask her how she knows me? No, I won't ask that question because that would be a discouraging start. Again, I got a message notification.

Do I know you?

How do I know if you know me or not? I thought to myself. When I was wondering what to respond, I received another message.

That's of course a stupid question. I should have asked whether you know me.

She sent a smiley with that message.

She's not that difficult to converse.

I'm not sure. I could tell if you tell something about yourself.

I waited for a response. No response came. I hoped I would get a response, but not yet. After a minute, she went offline. There goes another attempt in vain. I'm very much used to failures with girls, but every time, it hurts the same. I went down to say hello to my parents, who were busy with their duties. My mother was busy cooking, and my father was busy reading the newspaper with a cup of coffee.

"Why don't you sleep for some more time? Look at you. You look like a zombie." my mother advised.

"Always sleeping with your phone. Look how weak you are. Why don't you get engaged in some sports?" My father did his part in imparting some morning wisdom.

"Alright, mum, alright, dad." I said and walked back to my room.

Why don't parents understand that we are not infants, to always be guided and instructed? Why don't they let us live our life the way we want to?

I was more frustrated because of my morning experience with the new Facebook friend. It has been more than 15 minutes since I had accessed my messenger. It was such a long break for me. I immediately swiped my phone lock open and noticed a few notifications. I ignored the WhatsApp messages and jumped to Facebook notifications. I saw unread messages waiting to be opened. I didn't waste a second in opening it. Immediately, my lips curved into a smile. It was my newfound friend. After all, I didn't fail yet.

Tell me about yourself, and I'll see if I know you.

What should I tell? Everything about me is splashed in my profile. I still told her all about me.

I appreciate your honesty. Though I don't know you, I'm glad to be your friend.

I felt proud about the compliment. But she gave me vague information about herself. How can a girl open up her personal details to a stranger? I reasoned. Our chat journey started since then. It would be fair to say that she monopolised my time. Every time she chatted with me, she did so in offline status.

I do not want other guys to pester me, that's why I do not appear offline.

Her reason made me proud. Our relationship grew stronger. I shared her my phone number, and we also started chatting through WhatsApp and voice calls sometimes. She was a college student, so she didn't have many financial resources, which sometimes caused her phone to get disconnected due to a lack of balance. I hated that break. Hence, with much insistence, I recharged her phone. I enjoyed hot phone talks with her. However, the calls would often be interrupted by phone calls from her parents and relatives, as she stayed away from them. I started to learn many things about her. She is from a modest background and is studying in a hostel. She has a large, closely-knit family. She was so friendly that she had many friends. Sometimes I wondered how innocent she is. She told me everything about her and believed whatever I said. She was very open to me.

You are so gullible. Why are you so open? Don't you hold any secrets?

Why should I hold any secrets? You don't hold any secrets from me, do you?

You believe whatever I tell. What if I lied to you?

I believe everything you tell, but won't believe if you tell that you lied to me. Remember, every relationship is based on trust.

I was surprised at her sincerity. Our relationship grew stronger. I spent so much time with her that my group conversation with my friends diminished, so much that I have even ignored notifications regarding their conversations. I very rarely visited my friends' group on WhatsApp whenever she was busy with her family. My friends started asking questions and complaining about me. I stopped the rare visits also. She completely monopolised my time. Time flew like dust in the wind. Within 3 months, I started to share many personal things which I never shared even with close friends. The distance between us became thinner and finally vanished. We never hesitated for anything. When she was in some crisis, she would frankly express to me like a true friend. Whenever I was in stress, I would naturally reach out to her. I recharged her phone every month, even though she refused it. She never asks for any help. I appreciated her for being so self-dependent despite being financially deficit. Once, on a lighter note, I complained that my ear is getting roasted due to my phone heat. She immediately sent me a Bluetooth headset. I was very moved by her act because she cared about me so much and she didn't care to spend money even when she was so short of money. But whenever I would think of sending a gift to her, she would deny outright. If I had the address where she stayed, I would have sent it, but she didn't let me know the address for the same reason. She often said that I was her greatest gift. Every day she reminded me how lucky I was.

As things progressed smoothly, I lost track of time. I slowly realised that I fell in love with her. It was such a beautiful feeling. I have read about it so far, but experiencing it for the first time. Of course, I had a crush on many, but never was my feeling reciprocated. Then, again, we have not categorically declared our love. Exchange of messages expressed our love subtly. I started to spend even more time with my phone. As days progressed, my dad's advice turned into warnings.

"What's happening with you? You are giving us a scare."

"You better take care of your health. You look to be in deep trouble if you continue your obsession with your phone."

I hated their indulgence. Old-fashioned parents who don't understand that they need to give some space to their children. The more they nagged, the more I restricted myself to my own space.

"This is how parents lose their children." I bitterly thought.

Whenever I had unpleasant thoughts, I'd ping her, and they'd disappear instantly. She is my saviour and angel. Our relationship was a smooth sail until one day when my beautiful dream was shaken. She abruptly stopped responding to my messages. She was generally offline as she hated being pestered by the online vultures. Hence, I didn't know whether she was annoyed with me or if she was in trouble. I didn't know whether she received my messages or not. She didn't respond to my calls. I was worried if something terrible had happened. That thought made my life terrible. I became like a crazy monkey with withdrawal symptoms. My father's comments and my mother's brooding made my life worse. I left my home and thought of visiting my close friend. It had been ages since I visited him. He was my best friend in college, but social networking brought us closer to each other in a virtual world. Hence, there was no need for physical contact. It made life easy. But strangely, I felt great relief when I met him after a long time. I spent some quality time with hearty laughter. I wondered how long it had been since he laughed loudly. I came back home with a light heart. Strangely, my father didn't give me his routine lecture. I was relieved. Once I entered my room, her thoughts clouded me again. This continued for a few days. One fine day, my phone alerted an incoming message. I least expected it to be her, but every time an incoming message alerted, I would jump at it. This time I was not disappointed. It is her.

'Sorry, I missed your messages all these days. Some trouble.' she messaged.

'I was happy that she messaged, but worried about her trouble.'

I immediately called her.

'What's your trouble?'

'Nothing so serious. Hey, by the way. I'm leaving for my town.'

'Oh, nice. So, when are you returning?'

'I'm not returning.'

'What? You still have your course to complete.'

'There's no more course. I have completed my course before the due.'

She said with a forced smile.

'What do you mean?'

'Well… They won't let me complete the course if I don't pay my fees. I guess my family can't afford any more.'

I was silent for a minute as I found myself in a tight spot.

'What do I respond to this? Should I let her go? Or should I offer to help? What help can I offer?' I pondered.

'I need to pack my things and get ready to leave.'

'When are you coming back?'

'Why would I be coming back? I have nothing to do here. And I'm not sure if we would be able to continue our chat once I leave. I must confess, you had been a good friend. You have a great life. Goodbye, my friend.'

'Don't say goodbye. You're not going anywhere.'

'How can I stay? They won't allow me to stay unless I pay the fees.'

'Why do you give up? There should be a way.'

'I'm fed up of trying. People love you until you seek any help from them. And when you do, they shut their door on your face. Fake people and fake love.'

'No one cares for me.'

'Don't say that. There are people who really care for you.'

'There is no one who cares for me.'

'Don't you think I do?'

'You are my friend, but I can't accept the help from you.'

'If I'm in some trouble, won't you help me?'

'Of course, I would. I'm a friend, after all.'

'If you accept me as a friend, you would also accept my help.'

'I can't say how lucky I am. When my family and relatives refused to help me, you are helping me like a true friend.'

'I am a true friend.'

'My mother will be glad to know that I will complete my graduation.'

For a few moments, I didn't realise I actually agreed to help her with the money. I only intended to console her but ended up committing to help her.

Did I commit in haste to help? I questioned myself.

I have never helped anyone monetarily. It took me two months to replace my father's broken spectacles. But I have instantly agreed to help a girl whom I knew through social networking with 1.2 lakh rupees. I wired the money in a week. I was glad that she was happy. Then again, I thought, I have helped a girl whom I have never met with so much money.

'Hey Jas, shall we meet sometime?'

'I'm busy with my exams.'

'I'm travelling to my town for vacations.'

'My mother is not feeling well.'

I heard all kinds of excuses from her. I decided not to take any more excuses.

'We are meeting this weekend at the forum mall.' I stubbornly suggested, to which she agreed.

'I'm going to meet my angel this weekend.' I rejoiced.

This is my first reciprocated love affair. I was nervous and excited. I waited for the weekend with utmost curiosity.

'Send me a picture of yours in the meantime.'

She sent a picture. She was so beautiful. She was not very comfortable with selfies; hence, she always got her pictures captured by someone else. Most of the pictures were candid pictures, which I liked very much.

I eagerly waited for the day I would meet my girl after a long time of online acquaintance.

The day arrived, and I prepared to meet her with my best looks. Happiness showed on my face. I arrived at our rendezvous a little early and purchased a beautiful bouquet and a pack of Cadbury's celebrations. When I looked around at the happy couples, I proudly declared that I was no longer a lonely stag. I checked my phone for any messages or notifications but found none that interested me. The time on my phone display indicated that I was still 20 minutes ahead. I also noticed that the phone was on low battery. I cursed myself for not charging the phone and prayed the battery would stay alive at least until she arrived. I have heard many times that waiting for a beloved is the most prolonged affair. I believed it's true now. I kept staring at the phone every minute but was discouraged by the progress of time. To escape the pain of anticipation, I tried to divert my attention with the help of my favourite pastime – video games. I moved to the game park and started playing my favourite Grand Theft Auto. The game always excited me. It took some time to get my mind on it, but once I did, I lost track of time. Suddenly, I was brought back to my purpose. I quickly retrieved my phone to check the time, but to my horror, the phone was switched off. I looked around to find a clock. When I spotted a digital clock at the entrance of the game zone, it shook me off my seat. It was 30 minutes past the appointed time. I quickly rushed to the meeting spot, but there was nothing that delighted me. Multiple questions swamped my mind.

Was she late?

Did she wait for me and then leave, annoyed?

Did something terrible happen to her that she was not able to make it?

I liked to believe that she is late. If anticipation of her coming was painful, the uncertainty of the status is hell. I wanted to call her immediately, but my phone battery is dead. I rushed to the nearest charging station and put my phone on charge. I couldn't wait till it could get charged enough to make one phone call. I switched on my phone and made the phone call while still on charger. She didn't respond to my call. I tried again and again, but she started to reject my calls. And finally, her phone was switched off. I was heartbroken. I removed my phone from the charger as I wouldn't need it anymore. I returned home with a heavy heart. I sent apology messages to her on WhatsApp and Facebook. I guess she was annoyed with a notion that I had made her wait. I didn't know how to explain to her. I don't even know her physical location. Her Facebook and WhatsApp status never revealed her presence. I reckoned she left me forever. I started to divert my attention from her by actively participating in the group chats. I also occasionally visited my best friend as I felt that physical contact offered some inexplicable solace. Several months passed, and I started to regain my normalcy. Once when I visited my friend, I saw that he was annoyed. I asked him the reason and offered to help. He then revealed that he met a girl online, and they fell in love.

'What's the problem in that?'

'You know she is staying in a hostel to pursue her graduation. Suddenly, she says she is going back to her town forever.'

Something struck me like a hammer.

'Did she say that she won't be able to chat with you anymore?'

'Yes, she did.'

'Is she leaving because she is not able to pay her fees?'

'Oh, yes.' my friend replied in wonder.

'And her family and relatives refused to help her.'

My friend stared at me without answering.

'You should have agreed to help her with the fees.'

He stared at me, jaw-dropped, and nodded in response.

When I narrated my story, he was shocked at the scam. The girl follows the profile of prosperous guys who would be interested in girls. She knows a genuine profile; anybody would. We normally broadcast each and every moment of our lives on social media. She traps them and extracts money from them. When she feels that her safety limits are breached, she would break contact. I'm not sure how many people were cheated by her and how many cheaters are there. We are victims of our own stupidity.

Tooth for a Tooth

The hot rays of the early afternoon sun shone through the partially drawn curtain blinds. The sun rays that caressed her face did very little to disturb her sleep. Daisy, the puffy white ragdoll cat, climbed onto her belly and meowed gently. Her hollow stomach shrunk in a vacuum. She opened her eyelids as if they were a couple of iron curtains. The whole room spun like a hazy wheel, while her head pounded like a tribal drum. She tried to move her almost paralysed body out of her cosy bed, but failed in the first attempt. She gently moved the cat off her aching belly and rose on her elbows, looking around as if she was on an alien planet. With a herculean effort, she set her bare foot on the floor. Although the sun shone in, the floor was icy cold, sending chills down her spine. It was not an easy walk to her coffee maker, which was no more than twenty feet away. She felt like she was wearing a pair of magnetic shoes and walking on a metal floor. As she walked to fetch her coffee, she unconsciously kicked the empty beer cans scattered on the floor. Carrying the steaming hot coffee, her legs involuntarily led her listless body to her favourite rocking chair. As she seated herself, her pet cat and ever-reliable friend Daisy quickly jumped onto her lap. The cute cat managed to bring a mild smile to her battered face as she reaffirmed that she was never alone. Gently fondling her mane, she sipped her coffee, her mind busy recalling an incident as her eyes stared at nothingness.

戉扥

Summer was always a season of celebration in her ancestral bungalow in Palakpur, a modest village which thrives on agriculture and animal husbandry. The village may be devoid of skyscrapers and expensive cars, but the green landscapes and the poised lake were a visual treat. The pure air was such an elixir, giving a fresh breath of life. The land that bore her childhood memories never failed to amuse her. Vasanth Vihar, her ancestral bungalow, is a symbol of respect for many neighbouring villages and it had witnessed innumerable disputes and petitions from the villagers, settled amicably by her grandfather who is treated as their leader. The family was treated with great respect by the villagers. Visiting her village was always like returning to her mother's lap; until the last summer. She had always cherished her village memories; until last summer. Yes, last summer. All the pleasant memories were marred by nightmares. All the respect turned into ignominy.

Vasanth Vihar was a 100-year-old, two-storeyed palatial bungalow with sixteen bedrooms, housing a huge family of 42 under one roof, headed by the grand old man of the house. It was a happy place. But as the members of the family started moving out for education, career, and other reasons, the bungalow lost its blissful charm. However, they made it a rule to have a family gathering during the summer, which made their union even more delightful. This year was even more special. A surprise was awaiting them. Whether it was a surprise or a shock was yet to be known.

"Vaishali…" screamed her paternal aunt.

The enthusiasm was nothing new to her, but something suggested that there was more than just an atmosphere of a get-together.

Vaishali lost her parents at the age of six. Her paternal aunt took her responsibility and groomed her like her own child. She was a free-spirited girl who liked to make her own choices. She moved out of the house under the pretext of building a career she was passionate about, but that was just a partial truth. She hated being bound by principles and traditions. However, being a guest for a short period allowed her to enjoy the treasure of her childhood nostalgia and maintain her freedom at the same time. Still, all the major decisions were taken by the old man of the house, which didn't affect her until then. This summer was going to give her a different experience: an experience that is bound to turn her life upside down.

"How are you, mausi?" she asked as she hugged her with the usual passion.

"Looks like you have started your stupid dieting. Look at the pile of bones wrapped in the skin."

"Come on, aunt, you are exaggerating too much."

"Forget it. You have come to your aunt. Leave it to her."

Vaishali always found a huge challenge at the dining table in the form of her aunt. She keeps stuffing more and more food onto her plate, that she won't have the scope for refusing. But she always loved her.

She was greeted by the rest of the family members, and the family union was like a yearly festival that she was quite accustomed to by now. She began to mingle with people of her age, which was a relief. Or was it?

"You are very beautiful, sister." her cousin complimented her.

"Thank you, Rinku."

"I see your beauty has increased multifold this time." commented another cousin and gave a mischievous wink.

She did not understand whether to take it as a playful comment or if there was something between the lines.

"Enough of your mischief. Let her go to her room and freshen up." her aunt came to her rescue, chasing the tormenting cousins away.

She walked to her room in deep thought. There was something about the strange behaviour she didn't like. They were all good friends of hers, but mystery was not her cup of tea.

Summer evenings were always filled with festive jubilation. She was always happy to be part of it. There was music, games, and lots of delicious savouries served. However, she felt that she was the centre of attention. Or was she in an illusion? She wasn't sure. But the special attention scared her.

After all the fun, a sumptuous meal was served. The dinner table does not allow any diet restrictions; hence, everybody had their stomachs full. Then again, the whole family settled on the lawn in clusters and had a fun time with gossips and shared their experiences for some time. As you know, in villages, people go to bed early, unlike city life. Everybody hit the bed by 8 pm.

Vaishali was the kind of person who slept late. Occasionally, she partied all night. She was a nocturnal animal. But the rules here were different, and she had to abide by them. She turned and tossed on her bed, trying to make sense of the strange behaviour of her cousins, but somehow, she felt it was better not to understand. She fell asleep amid a quandary.

The next day, she woke up after everyone else, although it was early by her metrics. The hustle and bustle around her was unusual. It looked like they were going to have some visitors. It was not common for them to have visitors during summer as it was completely reserved for family. Everybody in the house was busy doing something. It looked like she was the only one who didn't do anything. But strangely, nobody asked her to do anything, which confused her even more. She stopped her aunt to enquire what was happening.

"Mausi, what's happening here?"

"Oh, my princess has woken up. Now get fresh, I'll serve you breakfast." she said and zoomed past her, shouting orders at the servants.

She was feeling hungry, but the suspense killed her hunger.

"Someone, tell me what the hell's happening here." she screamed within herself.

She thought it's better to get out of the place when no one's going to answer her questions. For the next few hours, the bungalow bustled with endless activities. When they gradually started to calm down, she started to comprehend the situation.

Before she completely understood the situation, she was engaged to someone she never knew.

"I'm really so happy for you, my kid." her aunt said with tears of happiness.

They are still the old-fashioned family roots who believe that every major decision should be taken by the head of the family. Her marriage was of paramount importance and pride to the family. And there were a lot of deliberations before they finally picked the groom who could uphold the family legacy. Everyone from the family knew about the arrangement, except her. Was it a surprise? Was it a tradition? She didn't understand. But what she knew was that they did not take the decision to hurt her. All the family gave her was happiness; so much that she never felt the loss of her parents. She didn't want to return the favour in this way. She had her own dreams and expectations.

There was a lot of buzz as the members of the family travelled back and forth because there was a lot of work to be done. The wedding was planned on short notice of two weeks during the summer weekend. It was short notice only for her, not for the family as it was planned before she arrived. The groom's family was invited over the following weekend. There were a lot of arrangements for food and entertainment for the guests. Everyone was jubilant. Summer weekends always evoked special interest in her, but not this time. As each moment passed, her heart beat rose with terrible fear of living her life with a stranger about whom she knew nothing. She wanted to do something to stop it, but she was not brave enough to openly declare it. With a lot of hesitation, she asked her aunt to allow her to talk to the groom for a few minutes. Though against the custom, she somehow managed to get the permission.

"You look so beautiful. The moment I saw your photo, I decided that I'm going to marry you." he told her with a proud smile, as if he had decided to buy a car or a farm.

"Well, I didn't get a chance to decide, you know?" her reply gradually faded his smile.

"Say, you are given a chance. What will your decision be?"

"We wouldn't have been here, then." she suddenly realised that she might be spoiling her chances.

"Sorry if my response was rude. I didn't mean to be offensive."

"If you don't like the wedding, why don't you cancel it before the engagement?" he asked in frustration.

"Well, things moved so fast that I didn't get time to react."

"What do you want me to do?"

"Without mutual consent, we can't have a happily married life. I plead with you to cancel the wedding." she finally unloaded what had been on her mind for a long time.

He thought for a few minutes, with unbearable discomfort.

"Well then, I don't want to live with a wife who doesn't like me."

She was happy that, finally, she was going to get out of the mental turmoil.

Her aunt observed that she was happy.

"Looks like you two have come to an understanding." her aunt asked with a smile.

She just nodded in delight and danced away, singing a jolly song. Her aunt was happy for her.

Days passed, but everything seemed normal. Vaishali began to panic as days passed smoothly. It was not long before the wedding day arrived. She was almost about to have a heart attack. The wedding mandap was being decorated, and the whole family was busy with the wedding tasks. She felt like she was lost in a mid-desert. She wanted to talk to the groom immediately, but it was not an easy task. In such a difficult situation, her aunt was the only person she relied upon.

She was in the groom's room with a flushed face, as she saw him smiling at her triumphantly.

"You said you'll stop the wedding…"

"I didn't say I won't marry you," he interjected before she completed the sentence.

"I said I won't live with a wife who doesn't like me. You will be my wife only when you like me. Until then, you'll be the daughter-in-law of the house."

She was shaken by the deceit. The cruelty of his intentions further terrified her.

'When she was not able to stand a dialogue for a couple of minutes with him, how will she live her whole life with him?' This thought forced some courage to bring the topic to her aunt as she was the only approachable person in such a situation. But the effort didn't bring reprieve to her. Although her aunt understood her situation and sympathised with her, she was not in a position to stop the proceedings at that stage. Vaishali, the free-spirited girl, was about to resign to fate that was imposed by her own family.

With a bowed head, she unwillingly walked down to the mandap, as the groom majestically sat with his head held high. As she sat beside him, she looked around at the huge crowd that had come to bless this one-sided affair. The Vedic chanting nauseated her, and her heart seemed to beat louder than the wedding music. At one sudden moment, she saw a couple of hands approaching her, holding a yellow sacred thread. She stood in reflex and stared at the bizarre atmosphere around her. Shock was written all over the hall. She then saw the fiery eyes of the groom commanding her to sit. She didn't budge. Unable to hold his temper any longer, the groom stood up and warned her through his clenched teeth, "Sit down in a moment."

When he realised that she was not going to give in, he shocked everyone with a hard slap across her jaw. Vaishali, who was not even admonished by her family, was slapped by a stranger in front of a thousand spectators. She clenched her teeth in anger, but it looked like he broke her tooth. In an unexpected moment, she returned a hard punch across his lower jaw, possibly breaking a tooth or two.

࿇

Although the wedding was called off, her act was unanimously disapproved by her family. Her aunt tried to play the peacemaker by explaining the cruel mindset of the groom, but it hardly made an impact. As she was walking out of the bungalow, she took a look back at the people whose faces were masked with anger. Her grandfather was not even willing to face her. But she knew that beneath his hard crust, there was a delicate heart that would never stop loving her.

She rubbed her jaw as she sipped her coffee. She smiled, despite her pain, as she recollected the terrible expression of the groom holding his cheek.

"It's called tooth for a tooth, ain't it, Daisy?" she said, caressing her mane and taking another sip of her coffee.

Love Googly

Her frizzy brown hair flowed a few inches below her shoulders, which complemented her long, lean face with a sharp chin and pointed nose. She never fancied wearing jewels, but her fair and flawless skin was adorned by the most beautiful smile I have seen. She never cared about her looks, but she looked so beautiful. I had known her since childhood, and she had been my best friend since then. She was an absolute tomboy. Football and cricket were her favourite sports.

My bond with her was so seamless that she thought what I thought, and my responses were a reflection of her thoughts. Our college believed that we broke the myth that a boy and a girl cannot remain friends beyond a certain level. I used to be very proud of that. But lately, I started feeling uneasy with that reputation. As I walked into the college canteen, she looked in my direction and nodded with a nonchalant smile, gnawing on the chewing gum. The dimple on her cheek will tell you what a beautiful smile that was. As I walked towards her, she kicked a chair towards me. She threw a pellet of her favourite chewing gum to me as I sat down.

"Hey, Chika. Cheerful day today." I greeted her.

"Yes, it is."

"What's with these punks? They sit all day without talking much, sharing a coffee, and staring into each other's eyes?"

"They are in love." I winked at her.

"So, what? I just don't understand what they get, blankly staring at each other!"

"Well, I guess it can only be understood when experienced."

"Well, well. Someone looks to have experienced love. Tell me, who is she? Do I know her? Is she from our batch? Tell me, tell me."

"Hey, Chika. If something like that happens, you'll be the first one to know. Trust me."

"You'll tell me before you tell the girl you love?"

"You bet."

"That's like my sweet Chiku," she spelled my name with pouted lips, gently held my cheeks in both her palms, and knocked her forehead gently on mine.

The nickname does not go with my name, but she still calls me Chiku because it goes with her nickname.

I returned a mock smile, but my mind studied her response to my love statement. I knew that she did not believe in love. But my heart ached when I saw excitement, instead of jealousy, in her voice to know the name of the girl I was in love with.

"Now, stop this stupid cuddly-cuddly nonsense. We have our college tournament starting next week. Got to win this for sure."

She's a part of our department cricket team. It was against the tradition to include women in men's team, but she's not the one who would take that nonsense. She lived up to the expectation. Her batting skills exceeded those of most of the men.

"Stop cribbing, boy, we've got it this time."

We lost the tournament in the finals to the computer science department by a whisker because we missed a crucial stumping. We lack a quality wicket-keeper. We belong to the mechanical department. She got admission for the computer science branch, but she chose Mechanical engineering. She chose it because everyone said that mechanical engineering was not meant for girls. She was the one who didn't like to be chained by the social opinions. She liked to prove that girls were no less than boys. I adored her for her strength and attitude.

"What's your plan?"

"We've got one lateral entry guy who joined our department last week. He's a wicket-keeper. Looks like he played for his college team."

"Oh, really!" I was excited to know.

"Oh, yes, he's really good. I've seen him a bit. I mean his game."

"Bad joke," I said.

I would have laughed with her for the joke a few weeks earlier. I didn't know when things changed.

It only takes a second to fall in love, but impossible to find that second. Love is a subtle affair that captures your heart without your knowledge, but conjures unthinkable changes. I was not a believer in love at first sight - Because, at first sight, it can only be physical attraction. Love is way far beyond that.

"Your mind is wandering a lot, Chiku." she said with a wicked grin.

"I was thinking about the match."

"Don't worry, I've got it covered, partner."

"Well… that's what I'm worried about." I said with mock fear.

"Catch this, lazy bones." she threw an empty coke can at me.

It hit me right on my head as I was not very good with reflexes. I picked it up and threw it back at her, which she effortlessly caught and threw it promptly into the trash can ten feet away. She's a far better player than me. Many times, in the past, my position in the team was debated, but she always ensured that I was part of the team.

"If he's not part of the team, there's no team. Mind it." she warned the team captain.

Ever since, nobody dared question my position, irrespective of my poor performance. She was my protector.

"We have our practice sessions every morning at six. Don't be a couch potato. Move your ass." she warned me.

"Stop butting me. You first work out on the short balls. Your helmet hits the ball more than your bat." I rebutted.

"Don't worrying about me. You know nothing but a sweep, and when you do, you sweep nothing but dust. You could hold a broom instead. You could, at least, clean the pitch."

"Then, play the tournament without me."

"Well, if that's what you want. Get lost. I'll find a better replacement." she said.

"Then, find one." I said, and left for my hostel room.

Such kind of petty quarrels were not uncommon between us. We fought twice every day, but it never once created a rift between us. However, I could sense something strange within. Many times, in the past, I boldly confessed my crush for girls in my college and also a couple of teachers. She once helped me propose to a girl, even though that affair didn't last long. She even commented that my affairs don't last long. True, it was. None of them made a lasting impression on me. I had easily confessed my love for other girls to her, but I couldn't express my love for her. My heartbeats spike whenever I think of expressing my love for her.

"What would she think of me? Would she think that I'm just like the other boys who couldn't maintain a dignified relationship with a girl? Is it a crime to fall in love with a girl who is your friend? Will I be able to remain the same old friend with her? Will

she abandon me if she knew that I have such a feeling for her? She doesn't need to abandon me; the thought of falling low in her eyes itself is devastating."

Innumerable questions hovered in my mind, not letting me sleep. After a long struggle, I slept. I didn't know when I fell asleep, but the constant ringing of my phone woke me up.

"I knew you would be sleeping, you lazy bones." I heard Chika scream on the phone.

I rubbed my eyes and looked at the table clock. It's 6 a.m.

"Didn't you find the replacement?"

"You are irreplaceable, my Chiku baby."

"I know." I said.

I knew that finding my replacement was the simplest thing for her, but she couldn't do without me. I prided in that.

"Now, slip on your shoes and move it."

"I haven't even brushed my teeth."

"Are you going to kiss someone?"

"Yes. You."

"You better use a good mouth freshener, then." she giggled.

"Now, move your ass. I want you here in 3 minutes." she said and disconnected the call.

I immediately jumped off my bed, slipped into my shoes, and gulped from a bottle of water as I rushed down the stairs of my hostel block. As I sprinted to the cricket ground, I saw her chatting with a new guy. I recognised him. He was Sameer, the lateral entry guy she mentioned yesterday. I slowed down my sprint and walked towards her. She looked in my direction, nodded, then continued chatting with him.

"He's the useless guy I had been talking about." she said, pointing towards me.

"Hey, I'm Sameer." he extended his hand to me.

"Karan." I shook hands with him.

"She calls you Chiku. I mean, your nickname doesn't go with your name."

"She doesn't have a sense of reasoning. That's why." I said.

"Take this." she said as she kicked my rear and started running.

"You're dead now." I started chasing her.

"Catch me first." she dodged me.

During the practice, I saw that he was as good as Chika said. We had a full-day training with intermittent breaks as it was a Sunday. By the end of the day, I was left with no energy.

"Catch you up for dinner." I told Chika and left for my room, dragging my foot.

Sameer hurried behind me and walked with me without much conversation.

"Quite a tiresome day, isn't it, Karan?"

"Ya, Sameer. Not many days for the tournament."

He followed me to my room.

"May I come in?" he asked.

"Sure." I said as I yanked my shoes off and switched the fan on.

"Can I ask you something?"

"Sure." I said. I didn't like him.

He hesitated for some time. I had a feeling he was going to ask some uncomfortable question.

"Are you in love with Ruchika?" Now, I really hated him.

"Yes, I love her." I simply replied, casually looking up at the ceiling fan.

He sat uneasily for some time, fidgeting with his phone.

"See you, buddy."

"See you, Sameer."

I saw disappointment on his face as he left, which pissed me off. My already disturbed mind further got annoyed by his curiosity. It's not difficult to understand his purpose for the questions. This guy is driving me mad. I had a long bath, fuming about the newfound menace. I laid down on my bed thinking about the events of the day. I didn't know when I fell asleep, but I woke up in the morning feeling rats in my stomach. I realised that I skipped my dinner. My phone showed twelve missed calls, all from Chika. The time on my clock showed 4 AM. I had a bottle of water and loitered along the corridor. It was dark outside, and cool breeze caressed my face. I didn't feel like sleeping. I walked to the terrace and looked in the direction of her hostel block. I checked my phone to see the timing of her phone calls. She had been calling me until 11 PM. I stared at the phone, wondering if she would also be awake. It was close to 5 AM. I gave up the idea. As I was loitering around the terrace, the ringing of my phone disturbed the silence of the wee hours. No one would call me at that time except her. I picked up the phone.

"What did you tell Sameer?" she straightaway asked.

My nerves froze with her question. My hands felt numb, and I feared I'd drop the phone. My heart beat soared. Without warning, she started to laugh aloud. She laughed continuously, and then she started to cough. I felt confused.

"Poor guy believed what you said."

I felt like jumping off the terrace.

"You should look at his face." she continued laughing.

"Why should he be worried about that?" I asked, and immediately regretted asking the question. I was a fool.

"You are right. Why should he be worried about that?"

I felt like that was a statement.

"Is he in love with me?"

"Only a stupid will fall in love with you."

"Maybe he is that stupid." she giggled.

"Stop your nonsense and let me sleep." I said and disconnected the phone.

I'm in love

She messaged me with a blushing smiley.

My heart broke into a thousand pieces. It's all my stupidity. The weather was no longer pleasant. I walked back into my room and banged my head on the pillow.

"What have I done?"

The next day at the college was like hell. I was late to the class. When I went to the college, my place was occupied by Sameer. They looked to be friends for ages. As I entered the class, she smiled at me and gave a naughty wink. She pointed to a seat behind her. I tried to act normal, but that was the most difficult task. I gave an angry stare and got seated as far as possible. She didn't seem to mind. She occasionally glanced towards me. I avoided her gaze by pretending to be busy jotting down the notes.

"You know what? He was grinning from ear to ear when he knew that we're just friends." she said, stuffing a piece of aloo paratha.

"Stop this nonsense. Our tournament starts this Saturday."

"Don't worry about that. Sameer's inclusion solves our wicket-keeping woes."

"All roads lead to Sameer!"

Avoiding his topic became a tough challenge for me thereafter.

The tournament started, and we progressed to the finals effortlessly. Sameer was the standout player. The final match was with the defending champions. They were not easy opponents. I noticed that, meanwhile, the friendship between Sameer and Chika started to grow deeper.

The final match was a tough one. We won the toss and elected to bat first. Sameer made 52 runs. The 90-run partnership between Chika and Sameer fetched us a total of 176 runs in sixteen overs. It was quite a defendable total, but the CS guys have a very good batting line up. They smashed our bowlers to the boundary almost every alternate ball. The score was 136/3 in 9 overs. The opponent captain, Rishab, was still batting on 71. There was no hope. In the following two overs, Rishab scored two massive sixes and a boundary. Their quick running between the wickets put a lot of pressure on the fielders who fumbled with the ball, allowing the opponent to convert singles into easy doubles. The opponent captain now reached 91 runs, guiding the team total to 163/3. The target looked like a piece of cake. Out of nowhere, our strike bowler Chandan ripped a hat-trick over for 3 runs which ignited our hopes. The score was now 166/6 for 12 overs. The team sprang back to life. The hat-trick over was followed by another tidy over of 5 runs and a wicket. The score now was 171/7 in 13 overs. 6 more runs required in 18 balls. There was a long discussion about who should bowl the next over. For me, it was totally hopeless as the opponent captain was batting at 95. The match was literally out of our hands. But our team is known for a 'never say die' attitude. The captain had to choose between Chika and Chandan. Finally, it was decided that Chika's spin trick would help the team. She spun the ball in her palm continuously, adjusting the field, shuffling the players, interchanging their positions. She was a leg spinner. She chose to lure the batsmen by offering a wide gap on the leg side. I was placed at the short fine leg position and a fielder was placed at the deep square leg. There was a wide gap between deep square leg and mid-on. She had two slips and a third man. The offside was further strengthened with a long on, point, and extra cover fielder. It was a perfect field set up for the tail end, as the captain was on the non-striker's end. Chika was a sharp turner of the ball. Everyone waited with bated breath as Chika hopped from around the wicket and pitched the ball a few inches outside the leg stump line, tempting the batsman to sweep the ball to the fine leg boundary. The trick worked as the ball sharply turned, grazing the top edge of the bat which was easily caught by the wicket-keeper. There was a loud cheer from the crowd.

"Chika, Chika, Chika." the crowd chanted.

Two more wickets to go, but only 6 runs to make. An odd boundary would finish the game as Chika has the tendency to bowl wide ball down the leg in an attempt of an expansive spin. Now the opponent captain and the new batsman had a long chat. Not a difficult guess. He wanted the strike. Chika pulled all the fielders closer. I was brought into leg slip position. The whole team was prepared to stop a single. It was such a tense situation. I prayed that the ball shouldn't come to me. She quickly galloped and bowled a similar ball, turning a huge margin from wide down the leg side. But the batsman managed to get a bottom edge in an attempted sweep, sending the ball towards me. I stopped the ball, but it spun to my chest. By the time I managed to get the ball in my hands, the non-striker already completed the run, but the batsman fumbled to reach the non-striker end. I quickly threw the ball to Chika, who ripped the bails in a flash. I was relieved that I was not going to be solely blamed for the team's loss. But again, I knew that though we stopped a single, I missed the golden opportunity to pick the captain's wicket. Our captain glared at me, but Chika waved him off. I breathed a sigh of relief. Now, the in-form skipper settled at the crease. The field was spread again, but eventually the same field setup. The two wickets seemed to be a very small achievement when he stood at the crease.

Chika didn't try any variation. The same ball was not going to trick the man in tremendous form. He swivelled the ball down between fine leg and the deep square leg for a boundary. 2 more runs to win. The batsman was one short of a century. Our captain sprinted towards Chika from the cover boundary and had a short chat. I guess he wanted to change the field, but Chika was stubborn. He can do nothing but shrug and walk back to his position. I was terrified that the ball would zoom in towards me. *Not again.*

Chika spun the ball in her hand and galloped with fiery eyes. This time she deceived the batsman with a flipper. The batsman didn't try too hard as he already had the game in his hands. All he had to do was to steal singles. That's what he tried. She pitched the ball outside the off-stump line from over the wicket with a slightly shortish length. He tried to play on the front foot and push the ball with the turn between point and extra cover. But the ball stayed low and straight, completely deceiving the batsman. The ball nipped the inside edge and flew towards the stumps. The ball just missed the stumps by a millimetre. The whole team had their hearts in their mouth. Just when we thought that the chance was lost, the wicket-keeper dived in and scooped the ball just a microsecond before it touched the ground. That was brilliant bowling. And terrific keeping, I should admit. The whole team and the audience roared in exuberance. Chika straightaway ran to Sameer and hugged him, almost lifting him off the ground. The team crowded around him. He was the star of the game. For me, it was Chika who contributed in all departments and won the match for us with an outstanding death over. But the excitement of a newfound wicket-keeper, which we lacked for a long time, made him a hero. Maybe, I was jealous. Deep down in my heart, I couldn't deny his awesome contribution. I saw him get rid of his gloves and lift Chika, who was screaming in frenzy. The jubilation was not a problem for me. What worried me was that she usually looked out for me whenever she was in joy, but she didn't even turn around to look for me.

"Maybe she did get a replacement for me." I thought sadly.

The whole crowd swarmed in. I silently slipped out of the crowd and walked straight to my room. I wanted to be alone. Everything seemed to work against me. I wanted to go somewhere. When the whole world is against you, there can't be a better place than home.

I switched off my phone and immediately packed my bag. I rushed out of the hostel as I didn't want to get embarrassed, caught with a brooding face. I'd die of shame if someone questioned me. I quietly slipped out of the campus.

∾

"What happened, baby? You look terrible." my mother asked.

She immediately found out something was not right.

"Just a little tired." I said, and went to my room.

Myriads of thoughts hovered around my mind.

"How can I expect someone to love me because I love her? She's not just someone. She's been a part of my life since my life began. How can I disrespect our friendship just because she's in love with someone else? Then again, I can't be the same friend to her anymore. Or can I? I should try. But it's not an easy job"

Thoughts kept tormenting me. I thought I could get rid of her thoughts in the home atmosphere, but there seems to be no place where her thoughts won't follow me. I tried hard to keep her out of my thoughts. I engaged in household tasks like gardening to get rid of her thoughts.

The next day, Chika came to my home with bloodshot eyes.

"Dear lord. What happened, Ruchi baby? You are scaring me." my mom cried.

"Where is Chiku?"

"What happened to you guys?"

"WHERE IS CHIKU?" she screamed.

"He's in his room." she replied immediately.

She knew something was terribly wrong.

I was in the shower when I heard crazy banging on the door.

"Who could that be?" I wondered, but I was in no mood to get out of the shower.

The banging turned violent.

"Is the house on fire?" I thought, wrapping the towel, slightly opening the door without turning off the shower.

The door was powerfully yanked open. I saw Chika standing at the door like a ball of fire. Without warning, she kicked me in my abdomen so powerfully that it brought me down to my knees.

"How dare you leave me alone?" she said, grabbing my hair.

"You were not alone, were you?" I said in a trembling voice, which infuriated her further.

She pushed me, and I fell on my back. Squatting on my belly, she grabbed me by my hair. She too got fully wet under the shower, but that couldn't camouflage her tears.

"I thought you found my replacement, after all." I said breathlessly.

"Don't ever say that. Don't you ever dare say that. There is no one in the world who can replace you. Many may come and go, but there is only one who would stay till the end. You are that one to me." She took a pause to catch her breath.

"When I turned around and found you missing, I felt myself missing from within. My life is incomplete without you. You are my friend. If I need to choose someone to love, you are my lover. And if I need to marry, you are my husband. You are my everything. My life without you is a meaningless book. I want you on every page of my book. I want you at every stage of my life. Don't leave me. Don't you ever dare leave me again. I want your love. I want to be your love."

"Only a stupid will fall in love with you." I said as I grabbed her hair, laughing in tears.

"Stupid." she said, and gently knocked her forehead on mine.

"Did you use mouth freshener?" she asked.

"No."

"It's okay… for this once." she said, trembling in tears of joy, and then she gave a passionate kiss on my lips. That kiss could be the longest kiss in history for me, as we lost track of time.

Author Quotes

Believe in your greatness because what you believe is what you become.

When you want something done badly, push yourself to a point of no return.

What has not happened could never have happened. But what can happen is in your hands.

You are never alone in your efforts: The universe is with you.

Perfection is nothing without persistent attempts to improve.

If your today is not better than yesterday, you have not done your best yet.

Anger is weakness. You need strength to be calm.

Be ambitious, but don't let your survival depend on your success.

Life will give you what you deserve. What you deserve depends on your deeds.

What has not happened could never have happened. But what can happen is in your hands.

Dreams are the blueprint to our destiny.

You fail not because you're not good enough, but because you haven't tried enough.

Growth is when you step out of your comfort zone.

Problems don't kill you. The fear of it does.

If you want luck, keep trying. Luck doesn't favour the idle.

If you can do it, but don't do it with the fear of failure, it's worse than not having any skill at all.

Power is not in your muscle, but in your determination.

Doing your best is more important than winning.

Nobody will give you anything. Nobody will stop you either. It's only you. Go get it.

Do what makes you feel good, rather than what you're good at.

Accept your limitations and work on your strength. Nothing can stop you.

When you don't resist unfavourable changes, you become what you don't want to be.

When you relish the pain of hard work as much as you enjoy success, there's nothing you can't achieve.

What is a life without dreams? What are dreams without pursuit?

Hatred hurts the one who bears it more than the one it's intended for.

Be focused on being correct, rather than proving others wrong.

Greed will deprive you of pleasure you have, against what you yearn to have.

Don't keep any thought in your mind that does no good. Your thoughts are seeds to your destiny.

When you try, you may fail or succeed. But when you don't, you have already failed.

You may lose a lot, but until you lose your self-confidence, you have lost nothing.

To achieve something great, you need skill. To achieve something impossible, you need guts.

When your heart is full of confidence, a miracle is always waiting to happen.

When you look into the eyes of the one you love, silence is the best music.

Working on something, despite certain failure, is better than sitting idle.

When you wait for the right time, you'll never know when it's already too late.

If you want to know your potential, test your limits. If you want to improve your potential, keep testing your limits.

If your today is not better than yesterday, you haven't done your best yet.

Don't worry about the past or the future. Just make your present count. It will take care of your past and future.

Being yourself is more important than being different.

When your common sense fails, your instincts will guide you. Follow your instincts.

Every act of goodness is born from our desire to be happy.

Depriving you of a pleasure you have never known, won't hurt you.

Evolution is when you don't make the same mistake twice.

You can't disown caterpillars if you love butterflies.

One who does not count the steps walks longer.

No matter how much you succeed, your life is meaningless when you can't spare a moment of joy with your loved ones.

When you have power and use it for a destructive purpose, you don't deserve it.

Perfection is a direction, not a destination.

I experience pain every day. The day I don't experience pain is the day I haven't tested my limits.

Just because miracles don't happen every day, don't rule out the possibility.

When you stop complaining about others for not helping you and focus on your efforts, there's no stopping you.

By being patient, you are favouring none but yourself.

If you won't do it now, you can do it never.

Happiness or sadness is a habit, not an emotion. Choose the better.

Sadness is not an excuse to do nothing.

Success discriminates against the sceptics.

You can't make others happy unless you are.

When you treasure what you have, you are already rich.

No matter how fast you run, you can't run into the future.

Everybody is nothing before they became something. Don't worry about being nothing. If you really want to become something, nothing can stop you.

Never underestimate anyone's power, especially yours.

There are two kinds of pains: One that you get out of working, and the other as a consequence of not working.

Half the world try to prove they are, what they are not. The other half refuse to accept what they are, they are.

Don't try to prove a point, just follow your heart.

You'll succeed if you do what you love. You'll fail if you sit idle. You're a failure if you love sitting idle.

Accept, analyse, and overcome your failures.

People like you for your likes, not for what you are like.

Your body has the strength to achieve what your mind resolves. If you can't achieve something, blame your mind.

You are not a loser when you lose, but when you give up.

You can't compete with a blind man in the dark.

Your dreams are what define you. Dream big. Chase your dreams.

Thank people who help you because they make you happy. Thank people who don't help you, because they make you strong.

When it's possible for you to dream, it's not impossible to achieve.

You can never finish your work unless you start. So, start now.

Don't care about success or failure. Keep doing what you love. Success will follow.

When you treat your failures as lessons, you can never fail.

The secret of success is to keep failing, but don't stop trying.

The biggest reason for failure is the fear of failure.

All good awaits those who persist.

Perfection is an outcome of uncompromising habit.

Don't keep things in your mind that don't do you any good.

If you are as good as others say you are, you are controlled by others' opinion. If you are as good as you think you are, you are in control of your life.

While you worry about the time you have wasted, you are wasting more time.

Your power is measured by your responsibilities.

You have not failed until you accept your failure.

Mistakes are not bad; excuses are.